PENGUIN BOOKS

A PRAIRIE HOME COMPANION:
The Screenplay

GARRISON KEILLOR is the host and writer of *A Prairie Home Companion*, the author of sixteen books, including the Lake Wobegon novels, and the editor of *Good Poems* and *Good Poems for Hard Times*. His syndicated column, "The Old Scout," is seen in papers coast to coast and online at Salon.com. A member of the Academy of American Arts and Letters, he lives in St. Paul, Minnesota.

Academy Award®–winning director ROBERT ALTMAN's more than thirty films include *M*A*S*H, McCabe & Mrs. Miller, The Long Goodbye, Nashville, The Player, Short Cuts,* and *Gosford Park*.

A Prairie Home Companion

The Screenplay

Story by
GARRISON KEILLOR and KEN LAZEBNIK

Screenplay by
GARRISON KEILLOR

Directed by
ROBERT ALTMAN

PENGUIN BOOKS

PENGUIN BOOKS
Published by the Penguin Group
Penguin Group (USA) Inc., 375 Hudson Street, New York, New York 10014, U.S.A.
Penguin Group (Canada), 90 Eglinton Avenue East, Suite 700, Toronto,
Ontario, Canada M4P 2Y3 (a division of Pearson Penguin Canada Inc.)
Penguin Books Ltd, 80 Strand, London WC2R 0RL, England
Penguin Ireland, 25 St Stephen's Green, Dublin 2, Ireland (a division of Penguin Books Ltd)
Penguin Group (Australia), 250 Camberwell Road, Camberwell,
Victoria 3124, Australia (a division of Pearson Australia Group Pty Ltd)
Penguin Books India Pvt Ltd, 11 Community Centre,
Panchsheel Park, New Delhi–110 017, India
Penguin Group (NZ), cnr Airborne and Rosedale Roads, Albany,
Auckland 1310, New Zealand (a division of Pearson New Zealand Ltd)
Penguin Books (South Africa) (Pty) Ltd, 24 Sturdee Avenue,
Rosebank, Johannesburg 2196, South Africa

Penguin Books Ltd, Registered Offices:
80 Strand, London WC2R 0RL, England

First published in Penguin Books 2006

1   3   5   7   9   10   8   6   4   2

Copyright © Prairie Film Productions LLC, 2006
Foreword copyright © Robert Altman, 2006
Introduction copyright © Garrison Keillor, 2006
All rights reserved

Photographs by Melinda Sue Gordon. Courtesy of Noir Productions, Inc.

"Gold Watch and Chain," words and music by A. P. Carter. © 1960 by Peer
International Corporation. Copyright renewed. International copyright secured.
Used by permission. All rights reserved.

"You've Been a Friend to Me," words and music by A. P. Carter. © 1941 by Peer
International Corporation. Copyright renewed. International copyright secured.
Used by permission. All rights reserved.

ISBN 0 14 30.3823 0
CIP data available

Printed in the United States of America
Set in Palatino
Designed by Sabrina Bowers

2

Contents

Foreword

A *Prairie Home Companion* is the product of Garrison Keillor's genius. He created it and nurtured it for thirty-some years before I got lucky enough to join him, along with our remarkable cast.

What a great chance this was. It was particularly dear to me because *A Prairie Home Companion* is radio, a medium I grew up on and plain adore. And because Garrison was such a generous host. (This is evident on his show: one of the program's great charms is that, every week, Garrison makes you feel entirely at home.) The film crew and I moved into the Fitzgerald Theater, from which the show has been broadcast for years, met Garrison's two stalwart actors of a thousand voices, Sue Scott and Tim Russell, his St. Paul sound-effects man, Tom Keith, and the musicians with whom he works every week, the formidable Guys' All-Star Shoe Band, and we went to work.

This script was the blueprint that guided us; its tone, its voice, is Garrison's. On the page you'll find characters that fans of the radio show have known for years (Dusty, Lefty, Guy Noir) and characters that Garrison created out of whole cloth for the picture (the Johnson Girls and Lola; the Dangerous Woman; the Axeman; and the very pregnant assistant stage manager, Molly). Garrison loves to tinker, and he retooled scenes as we shot, endlessly responding to our progress (or lack of same), to what happened the day before, to our cast. But what he did first—and it's evident here from page one—is cast a spell. A script is a kind of incantation that summons up a world and that suggests a way to proceed. We were so fortunate in making this picture, most notably in our spectacular cast, and in the almost unreasonable amount of fun we had working together. Our luck started here.

—Robert Altman

Introduction

Moviemaking in the Radio Business

I wanted the movie to be called *Savage Love* and have Palominos in it and the Mississippi and lilacs and a violinist named Lil. I hadn't fleshed out all the details, just the basics—"She didn't want to go to him. She knew how it would end. And yet she was intoxicated by his voice on the phone when he said 'Why don't you slide on over here and bring your fiddle?'—she repeated it to herself as she rode Beauty along the riverbank and galloped the last hundred yards and gracefully cleared the lilac bushes and landed in his front yard."—but as you may know by now, I lost that argument. Mr. Altman wanted to make a movie about life backstage at a Saturday night radio show, so that is what I set out to do.

I've been doing a Saturday night radio show called *A Prairie Home Companion* since 1974, as it so happens. It began as a knock-off of *The Grand Ole Opry* in Nashville and since has transmogrified into a loose amalgam of the Opry, Fred Allen, *Lux Mystery Theater, Let's Pretend,* and Bobby Benson and the B-Bar-B Gang. It started in April 1974, in Minneapolis, at the Walker Art Center, under the sponsorship of Suzanne Weil, and went on the air in August over Minnesota Public Radio in St. Paul. It's been around ever since, except for a three-year sabbatical in the late eighties.

The name of the show comes from a cemetery in Moorhead, Minnesota, established in 1875 by the Norwegians who had settled there in the Red River Valley. They had expected to stay for a few years, make some money, and then return to Norway, or go on to California, or Oregon, or any place other than this godforsaken, windswept, treeless plain, but then a young lawyer named John Elmer drowned in the Sheyenne River, and his brother Oscar decided not to ship the body back East to New York where the two of them had started out but to bury it in Moorhead. John had suffered from "nervous difficulty" and his brother suspected suicide. Somehow this tragedy made up Oscar's mind to stay—Norwegians can be contrary that way—and he founded Our Prairie Home Cemetery and put his brother in it.

This story appealed to me—Norwegians establishing a graveyard as a sign that they intended to stick around—so I took the name and stuck "Companion" on it as a dark joke. Radio was sort of my Moorhead. I hadn't much respect for it. I thought radio people were pretty glib and shallow. I was a writer, not a performer, and radio announcing was a temporary day job until I could finish a novel. I had one in the works about a small town in Minnesota, but it languished and then I lost the manuscript in the train station in Portland, Oregon. And meanwhile I went to Nashville and sat in the balcony of Ryman Auditorium and watched the Opry, the ladies in sequins, the red-barn backdrop, the haze of cigarette smoke, the flashbulbs, the announcer in his funeral suit, and decided to steal the idea and transplant it up North. A haphazard career choice. I had no idea what I was getting into, and that was good because I had poor judgment: if I'd thought harder, I would've made the wrong decision. Only impulse could have saved me. And the impulse to start up a show as complicated as this, with musicians and an audience and all, was my way of telling myself that I intended to settle down in radio and not move on.

Of course there were Hollywood temptations along the way. In 1985, the book *Lake Wobegon Days* was published and director Sydney Pollack invited me to write a screenplay and we tramped around small towns in Stearns County for a few days, talking about moviemaking. (He talked and I listened.) It all seemed so easy. For a year afterward, I tried to write scenes based on the book and everything fizzled. Five years later, the director Patricia Birch asked me to write a screenplay based on a monologue from the radio show about a boy who loves a rock 'n' roll band called Mammoth, and that project went into development at Disney for a couple years and then sank when a big executive left the company. He was our patron and we got dropped. Miss Birch then took the idea to Miramax and I got to sit in a tiny office in Tribeca and pitch the story to Mr. Harvey Weinstein, who did not crack a smile. The story was hilarious when I walked into the room and then became dramatically less so as I told it to him.

A few years later, the director Michael Winterbotham invited me to write a screenplay version of my novel *Wobegon Boy* and I did and it was much less faithful to the book than he wanted it to be and that project faded to black. Three movie projects, zero movies.

And then Mr. Altman came along with his idea of writing a back-stage drama. He came to see a few shows—one in New York, one at a big Methodist tabernacle in Ocean Grove, New Jersey, and one at the Fitzgerald Theater in St. Paul—and that, for some reason, convinced him that there absolutely was a movie here. He loved the band, the show's actors, the sound-effects man, the semi-chaos onstage, the stagehands coming and going. All that was needed was a script. "And that," he said grandly, "I leave to you."

Life backstage at *A Prairie Home Companion* is hardly a maelstrom of bitter conflict and raw emotion. Minnesota is a state of low-maintenance people and everyone backstage has a job to do and there isn't time for big scenes. We've had our share of big stars on the show—Taj Mahal, Renee Fleming, Randy Newman, Willie and Percy Humphries, Faith Prince, Doc Watson, Sam Bush, the Fairfield Four, Manhattan Transfer, the Juilliard String Quartet, Bryn Terfel, Spider John Koerner, Sarah Jessica Parker, Leo Kottke, the Everly Brothers, Yo-Yo Ma, Chet Atkins and Jethro Burns, Midori, Willie Nelson—but I don't recall anybody stalking around and pitching a fit. One time the piano was locked and we had to find a janitor. A couple times, the power has gone out. There have been intoxicated musicians. There have been love affairs. There have been blizzards. One in Birmingham, Alabama, as a matter of fact. Once a boy in the first row threw up during my monologue. He was sick, his mother explained to me later.

I wrote a first draft in which a radio show is being filmed by a documentary crew who brings in a truckload of gear and whose lights blow a fuse at the theater and meanwhile the radio show goes on in the dark. This appealed to me—a blackout in a movie—but not to Mr. Altman. I wrote another draft in which a singer who has gone on to become a big star writing cheesy patriotic anthems returns to the show and whom the stagehands consider a jerk and try to sabotage. And then I created a couple of singing sisters, the Johnson Girls, who are the remnant of a larger sister act and who have survived a series of mishaps in the music business. I sent the script to Mr. Altman who said, "I think you've got something there." And before I'd written much more, he'd talked Meryl Streep and Lily Tomlin into playing the roles. "Meryl is a terrific singer," he said. "And Lily will learn."

Mr. Altman was a very courtly collaborator. Writing was my business, he said, and he kept his comments to a minimum. His business was casting. I took the detective Guy Noir (whom I play on the real *Prairie Home Companion*) and made him a character in the screenplay, a security man, and Mr. Altman considered a number of actors, looking for a heavyset one, and suddenly the elegant Kevin Kline walked into the picture. I brought in the radio cowboys Dusty and Lefty and Mr. Altman chewed on that for a while. And then Lindsay Lohan lobbied him for a role and he said yes, though I hadn't written one for her yet—I guess it's called pre-casting—and one day I read in the paper that she'd said in an interview that she'd be playing Meryl Streep's daughter. So I created a daughter, named Lola (after the character in *Damn Yankees* who sings, "What Lola Wants, Lola Gets"). I am the sort of writer who thrives on assignments. A blank slate makes me crazy, but if you tell me what you want and give me a deadline, I'm happy.

The script kept changing through the fall of 2004 and the winter—I added a singer named Chuck Akers, which was a name Chet Atkins used on the road to register under at hotels, and I had him die backstage. (I remembered our old drummer Red Maddock telling me backstage, with a big grin on his face, that he hoped he would die while he was playing, and I remembered my horror at the thought.) I had a character called Dangerous Woman who started out a crazy listener who thought the announcer was in love with her and turned into an addled songwriter auditioning for a spot on the show and then—lightbulb lights!—the angel of death, a beautiful woman who is sometimes visible to other characters, sometimes not. "Okay to put a supernatural being in?" I e-mailed Mr. Altman. "Okay, but no special lighting effects," he replied.

Over the winter, the script got to where Mr. Altman felt he was ready to shoot it, and then his production company set out to look for investors. He is an independent who has worked in big studios and outside of them, plowing forward no matter what, surviving his successes, weathering the exigencies of the trade, defying movie business trends, and now the real job began—finding people who wanted to invest five or six million dollars in a script written by an amateur for an eighty-year-old director. Meanwhile, I kept revising. I put in more songs, more radio commercials. I put in the announcer, pulling his pants on, trying to tell a story about how he got into radio and being interrupted by others. (I wrote the part for George Clooney who I thought was interested and who moviegoers would have enjoyed watching put his pants on, but Mr. Altman let me know that he had cast me in the role. "People will be disappointed if you're not in it," he explained. I explained that other people might be disappointed if I was in it. He prevailed.)

Mr. Altman kept casting the parts from New York as the characters popped up—and late in the game, I figured out how I could get my pals into the movie. I wrote them in by name. (Duh.) For example:

ROBIN and LINDA join GK onstage.

GK
Hey.

ROBIN & LINDA
Hey yourself.

Or words to that effect. And New York asked, "Who they?" "Robin and Linda Williams," I said. "Are those characters or are those real people?" New York asked. "Both," I said. I did the same with Jearlyn Steele.

I was still rewriting the screenplay when Mr. Altman and his crew moved into the St. Paul Hotel in June 2005 and truckloads of camera and lighting gear started unloading in the alley behind the Fitzgerald Theater. I had done a wheelchair version of the script a couple weeks before when it appeared that Meryl Streep, after recent knee surgery, might not be ambulatory, and then she called to say she was fit and ready to dance, so I dehandicapped the screenplay, and then Mr. Altman decided to add a noirish opening scene at Mickey's Diner with Kevin Kline doing a voice-over, so that needed to be written, and meanwhile the crew was turning our old theater into a studio, laying down tracks for the cameras and setting up a big camera boom and getting ready to start shooting. Mr. Altman did not flinch when I told him that I still had some changes to make, though one of the producers blanched. I'd never made a movie before so I had no idea that you couldn't keep on changing things right up to the last minute. But Mr. Altman, who had made a lot of movies, didn't know you couldn't do that either.

I met Meryl Streep and Lily Tomlin at the Fitzgerald the Sunday night before shooting started. They had been rehearsing songs and they wanted me to hear them. Meryl wore a red skirt and poofy white blouse and Lily was in jeans and denim jacket. They claimed to be nervous and flounced around and got all girlish and then launched in. Meryl sang lead, Lily alto, and the harmonies were the duet harmonies I remember from church. It was stunning to watch them do this and to think that actors were going to bring to life all of this stuff I'd written. It made me want to go back and rewrite the whole thing.

I left town for a week's tour out East with the radio show and got daily reports on how well the first scenes with Meryl and Lily and Lindsay Lohan had gone, which I distrusted. People in show business are always telling you how great something was when you yourself know it was only marvelously adequate.

When I got back to St. Paul, a makeup trailer was parked on Exchange Street and a commissary wagon where you could walk up to a window and order an omelet and pour yourself a cup of coffee. And there, sitting on the steps, eating breakfast, were a dozen old pals of mine from early radio days who had been signed up as extras in the movie. Old veterans of the Powdermilk Biscuit Band and the Brandy Snifters and Peter Ostroushko and Butch Thompson. I walked into the theater and the lobby was a warehouse of lighting gear and camera tracks and the prop master had set up shop in the atrium. Production assistants were buzzing around, and one of them led me upstairs to a dressing room and there was my black suit and white shirt and red tie and red socks and shoes. She handed me three pages of script, the day's shoot, and there was my name. As an actor. My debut (gulp). And a sort of chasm opened at my feet. *You could* (I thought to myself) *become a synonym in the movie business for One Who Makes a Fool of Himself.*

The next four weeks went quickly. I got to sing a duet with Meryl, which I foolishly looked at on video playback—she is luminous, beautiful, bursting with cinematic feeling, and I look like a guy brought in off the street as a stand-in—and while I was recovering from that, she grabbed me by the hand and danced me around and planted a smacker on my lips. I did a scene with Lindsay in which she rose from a chair and walked over, her eyes brimming with tears, and accused me of being a jerk. I had written her lines but nonetheless she made them sting. We did the scene six times and each time her eyes brimmed and the lines stung me to the quick. I did a nice scene with Virginia Madsen in which I chewed an apple. Kevin Kline admired my chewing and felt it was evocative and, in its own way, brilliant. And almost every day I reported to the Fitzgerald with rewritten scenes in hand. "Are those for today?" the producer said, turning white. "Bob asked me to do it," I said, which was a lie, but I'm good at that, having had years of practice. So the changes got put in.

One day Lindsay handed me the shooting script for the next day and said, "You aren't going to make me say all that, are you?" She was right: I'd stuck her with a whole page of exposition, a big lump of essay. So I went home and rewrote it into a scene. She was happy. They shot it. It went well.

It's unprofessional for the screenwriter to lurk around a movie shoot and snatch scripts out of people's hands and scratch out lines and write in new ones. A movie shoot is like an invasion and requires vast detailed planning in order to get the work done on time and stay on budget. The last thing a director needs is a screenplay that keeps changing. But who said I'm professional? Not me. And once you get on a set and see how the actors move and what a scene looks like on film, you learn things about your story you couldn't have figured out sitting in a dim room with your laptop. And so I kept revising. A scene disappeared, in which Meryl and Lily and Kevin and I are walking down the street in the dark after the show, looking at the Fitzgerald over our shoulders, the back doors open, light flooding out, Lindsay inside onstage dancing. It would've taken hours to set up, hours to shoot, and it added nothing to the story. Out it went. In between scenes, Kevin sometimes sat and played the piano, which he does rather well, so I wrote him a scene in which Guy Noir sits and noodles and sings a few lines from Robert Herrick, with a bust of F. Scott Fitzgerald on the piano. Why not?

The last thing to get written was the title. The working title through the end of the shoot was *The Last Broadcast* and then, months later, Mr. Altman told me that he would prefer to call it *A Prairie Home*

Companion. But that's the name of my radio show, I said. In the movie the show dies. In real life it continues, Lord willing. I wouldn't want the show's audience to be confused about that. The show ended once, back in 1987, and once is enough. "I just like the title," said Mr. Altman. We were sitting in his office in New York with all of his movie posters on the walls—*Nashville*; *M*A*S*H*.; *McCabe & Mrs. Miller*; *The Player*; *Gosford Park*; *Come Back to the Five and Dime, Jimmy Dean, Jimmy Dean*; *Popeye*; *Cookie's Fortune*; *Kansas City*—and midtown Manhattan out the window and he was halfway done with editing the thing and feeling pleased with it so far and apologetic about some good stuff he had had to cut. That was a new experience for me, being apologized to by a famous movie director for snipping out some dialogue of mine. I was touched. "Okay by me," I said. And that was the end of it. And now it's in print and this really is the end of it.

People ask me if I like the movie and of course I say yes. There are so many fine acting turns in it, wonderful stuff to look at, and Mr. Altman knows how to make a movie move. But I would love to rewrite the whole thing. Sometimes I imagine it's 3 AM on a Sunday morning in July, the crew is shooting at Mickey's on St. Peter and 7th Street in downtown St. Paul, a stagehand is hosing down the street, Bobby is working the big boom camera, Vebe is marshaling everybody for the next take, Mr. Altman and his wife Kathryn are watching a video monitor, Meryl Streep has just kissed everybody good-bye ("I don't want you to have any fun without me!" she cries), and now Kevin is rehearsing a Hopperesque scene, sitting at the counter of the diner, walking to the cash register, putting on his hat, coming out the door, striking a match, lighting a cigarette, and walking across the rain-streaked pavement toward the camera. No dialogue. But I imagine him saying to me, "Write me a line." And I do. I'd be happy too. Let me sit down here for a minute with a pencil and paper and I'll come up with something.

—Garrison Keillor

A Prairie Home Companion

The Screenplay

OPENING TITLES

A still picture of Minnesota countryside with a radio tower, its beacon flashing.

> RADIO VOICES (OFF CAMERA—O.C.)
> Market reports today: barrows and gilts 220
> to 260 pounds are lower at 40 dollars. Sows
> are steady 300 to 500 pounds, 34 to 37 dollars.
> Going over to the feeder cattle . . . beef steers
> 120 to 150 dollars are 200 to 300 . . .
> (FADES)
> The way I like to do it is I take one can of
> cream of mushroom soup and then one
> package of egg noodles. I like the egg
> noodles better than the Italian ones. I like to
> put . . .
> (FADES)
> If we look at what the Lord said in the Book
> of Revelation . . . you can be sure that there's
> a price to pay for the way of the flesh . . . and
> that price will be paid . . .
> (FADES)
> And here's the windup and the pitch. And
> it's . . . two and two, two and two . . .
> (FADES)
> Before you just say, Honey, I think we have to
> have some couple's counseling, I mean . . .
> we have problems, I can't leave a cup there
> for . . .
> (FADES)

RADIO VOICES (O.C.) (CONT'D)
All right, it's time for traffic on the fives and
let's find out what's going on with your
drive. Let's go to Chopper. Chopper, what's
happening?
(SEGUES TO)
Alright, we got a fifteen-minute wait at 494:
there's an accident working at the spaghetti
junction. 694/Silverlake Road a very slow go.
Back to you . . .

1   EXTERIOR (EXT.) DOWNTOWN ST. PAUL—NIGHT

The Cathedral of St. Paul, lit, on a high hill over the city, a
grand Romanesque dome with cupola beacon. The camera
pulls back from the dome to a rain-slicked sidewalk on a
downtown street, traffic passing, and cranks around to show
Mickey's Diner, a railroad-car diner with bright marquee,
windows lit, and a lone patron at the counter, GUY NOIR, in
profile, drinking coffee, a counterman scraping the grill, back
to the camera.

GUY NOIR (VOICE-OVER—V.O.)
A quiet night in a city that knows how to
keep its secrets, but one man is still looking
for the answers to life's persistent questions.
That's me. Or it used to be.

GUY NOIR stands and picks up the check, fishes in his
pockets for money to pay.

GUY NOIR (V.O.)
It was a rainy Saturday night in St. Paul and I
had just finished off a grilled cheese
sandwich with beans for a chaser and it was
time to head for work across the street.

2   EXT. DOWNTOWN ST. PAUL—NIGHT

GUY NOIR emerges from Mickey's Diner and crosses the wet pavement toward the camera.

> GUY NOIR (V.O.)
> I'm a private eye. Noir's the name. Guy Noir.
> But I had taken temporary employment
> about six years before doing security
> for a radio show called *A Prairie Home
> Companion*—on account of a serious cash-
> flow problem due to a lack of missing
> heiresses and dead tycoons lying in the
> solarium with lipstick stains on their
> smoking jackets. In other words, I was broke.

CUT TO:

3   EXT. DOWNTOWN ST. PAUL—NIGHT

GUY NOIR walking north on Wabasha, turns right at the corner and we see the marquee of the Fitzgerald Theater. He stops.

> GUY NOIR (V.O.)
> This radio show was done out of an old
> theater called the Fitzgerald and it'd been on
> the air since Jesus was in the third grade but
> it was still pulling in a few hundred people
> on Saturday nights. It was a live radio variety
> show, the kind that died fifty years ago, but
> somebody forgot to tell them. Until this
> night. A big corporation down in Texas
> had bought up the radio station and their
> axeman, a guy named Cruett, was on his way
> to St. Paul to shut the thing down and turn
> the theater into a parking lot. It was curtains
> and everybody knew it but nobody said so.

GUY NOIR (V.O.) (CONT'D)
They were Midwesterners. They felt like, if
you ignore bad news, it might go away. Not
my philosophy, but I'm not from here. Stay
on the edge of the crowd, keep your eyes
open, that's my motto. It was my last night of
gainful employment for a while and I had a
feeling it was maybe going to be interesting.

4   EXT. FITZGERALD THEATER—NIGHT

A lively four-hand piano piece, "Dr. Wang," FADES IN:

As GUY NOIR wends his way through the crowd in front of
the Fitzgerald, standing, talking, smoking, waiting for friends.

WOMAN (V.O.)
I thought she was older than that.

2ND WOMAN (V.O.)
She is older. Those pictures are retouched.
Airbrushed. All of them.

The camera pans picture posters on the front of the theater, of
Yolanda and Rhonda Johnson, Chuck Akers, Dusty and Lefty,
Garrison Keillor, and Jearlyn Steele.

WOMAN (V.O.)
I didn't know they did that.

2ND WOMAN (V.O.)
Yeah, they all do that. They always did.

5   INTERIOR (INT.) FITZGERALD WINGS—SAME TIME

The stage, viewed from above. The front curtain is down. A
row of six microphones downstage, and an announcer's
lectern with a microphone hung over it. A stagehand is taping

down the microphone cords. At the piano sit two pianists, one in tuxedo and one in jumpsuit, playing "Dr. Wang"—the show's pianist and a stagehand. Musicians are assembling, arranging sheet music on stands, standing in little groups, talking. Four stagehands wheel the large Prairie Home house set into place as a Powdermilk Biscuit drop is lowered into position over the piano. A production assistant is setting out music on the music stands of the bandstand. A guitarist is tuning. A woman comes out with an armload of music and sets it on the piano as the musicians play.

6   INT. FITZGERALD WINGS—SAME TIME

CHUCK AKERS stands in the wings, in jeans and a cowboy shirt, holding a guitar by the neck, facing us.

> CHUCK AKERS
> Would you mind taking my picture?

He hands a small digital camera past the camera and poses for a moment.

> CHUCK AKERS
> —It's the button on the front.

He poses, smiles. There is a flash.

> CHUCK AKERS
> Thanks. Take another one. —Hey, Evie! Come over here. Come on, angel. Don't fuss about your hair.

The camera pans quickly to the LUNCH LADY standing nearby, who ducks, covers her face. She is short, plump, fiftyish, in jeans and an apron. A STAGEHAND standing next to her takes her by the shoulders, preventing escape.

> CHUCK AKERS (V.O.)
> Come here and take a picture with me and
> make my wife jealous.

CHUCK AKERS and the LUNCH LADY stand side by side, his arm around her shoulder, her arm around his waist, smiling, in the flash of a camera.

> STAGEHAND 1 (V.O.)
> I've told these people a hundred times not to
> yank on the microphone—if you want to take
> it off the stand, you squeeze the clip, the
> microphone comes right out—and what do
> they do? Yank on it.

7   INT. FITZGERALD THEATER—SAME TIME

STAGEHAND is replacing the clip on a microphone stand.

> STAGEHAND 1 (CONT'D)
> The clip works fine if you squeeze it. How
> hard is that? You yank on it, you're gonna
> bust it.

He finishes his repair and walks away.

> STAGE MANAGER (ON P.A.)
> Ladies and gentlemen, the house is open and
> this is your fifteen-minute call. Fifteen
> minutes to showtime. Fifteen minutes.

The STAGE MANAGER, a tall man in an ill-fitting suit, clicks off the intercom mic. He stands at a large illuminated lectern, just behind the proscenium. It is almost as big as a drafting table. This is the command post for the broadcast. A large black leather-bound script book lies open on it. Phone numbers are scrawled on it, Post-it notes are attached, a wiring schematic. Two black telephones are attached to the side of it and an outline of the show, written out in Magic Marker, is taped to the wall above it. A gooseneck lamp extends down from the wall, too, and a big studio clock, analog, with a bright red second hand, and a digital countdown clock. His assistant, MOLLY, stands next to him. She is young and pregnant.

STAGE MANAGER
How many duct tapes I got?

MOLLY
Two duct tapes, one Powdermilk Biscuit, a coffee, a ketchup, and the Federated Association of Organizations. That's the first half hour.

STAGE MANAGER
Where's the announcer?

MOLLY
He's in makeup.

STAGE MANAGER
About fifteen years too late. Where's my pencil? I just put it down here.—Don't stand up close to me, okay? Sorry. I don't like to be crowded. I'm like a rat in a coffee can as it is.

(TO SOMEONE IN THE DISTANCE)
Don't leave that there!!! Get it out of there!!!—Jesus.

MOLLY
It'll be just fine, Al.

STAGE MANAGER
I spend my life looking for a pencil I had in my hand ten seconds ago—

MOLLY
It's in your pocket. Right here.

STAGE MANAGER
Don't crowd me. Okay?—Could we get a
band onstage? What do we have to do—send
out engraved invitations or what?

He reaches into a drawer for a bottle of antacid tablets, shakes
out a handful, chews them. CHUCK AKERS looks over his
shoulder, in a cowboy shirt and hat, jeans, boots, a cigarette
dangling from his lower lip.

CHUCK AKERS
What segment you got me in, Al?

STAGE MANAGER
Got you in the first ten minutes, Chuck. No
smoking, okay?

Beyond his desk, a little group of musicians laugh out loud,
someone having just told a joke.

STAGE MANAGER
Keep it down, wouldja!!

STAGEHAND 2 crosses the stage in front of the bandstand, a
ragged semicircle of music stands, microphones, and stools
around the piano. The drummer climbs into his nest of drums,
runs through some drum warm-up riffs, as a mandolinist with
a fiddle under his arm walks onstage. MOLLY crosses the
stage, wearing a headset, an armload of papers in hand, some
under one arm, some held in her mouth, passing out sheets
to members of the band, stagehands, collating as she goes.
Musicians circulate in the wings, tuning, talking, primping in
a mirror, playing.

The audience can be heard as it arrives in the house.

STAGE MANAGER (O.C.)
Molly? Get Dusty and Lefty up here.—Would
you mind carrying on your love life
somewhere else? Huh?

STAGEHAND 2 (O.C.)
Al, can we do something about people
yanking the microphones out of the clips?

STAGE MANAGER (O.C.)
Don't talk to me, okay?

CUT TO:

8   STAGE—CONTINUOUS

STAGEHAND opens the curtain slightly and we see through
the crack the audience filing in, milling, moving to and fro, the
seats about half full.

LEFTY (O.C.)
How long you been doing this?

GARRISON KEILLOR (GK) (O.C.)
Doing what? Taking off my pants?

LEFTY (O.C.)
How long you been doing radio?

GK (O.C.)
Oh. Well—

CUT TO:

9   INT. MAKEUP ROOM—SAME TIME

A big mirror with pictures taped to it. Makeup supplies on the
table under it, which is also crowded with pictures in silver

frames, a coffeemaker sitting on a microwave, phone books, a stuffed cat, a snow globe, a No Parking sign. There are hand-lettered signs, too: "DO NOT 'HELP YOURSELF' TO MAKEUP. ASK FIRST. THIS MEANS YOU." "COFFEE 25¢— ASK ABOUT OUR WEEKLY & MONTHLY RATES."

GK stands in the middle of the room, in white shirt, undershorts, red socks, holding a pair of pants, which he is hanging on a hanger. LEFTY sits at a table playing solitaire. DUSTY slouches in a chair, thumbing through a magazine. Other musicians come and go. DONNA, the makeup lady, works on a musician sitting in the makeup chair, at the mirror. GK's dressing area is a corner of the room, his black suit hanging on a hook, his shoes, an old black Underwood typewriter on a stand, with stuff piled on it.

> GK
> I don't know. Thirty years. No, forty. They
> were having Mark Twain Days on the
> Mississippi and I was hired to dress up as
> Huck Finn and run a raft and take people for
> rides and one day the raft hit the wake of a
> steamboat—

MOLLY enters.

> MOLLY
> Mr. Keillor, we need you onstage—

> LEFTY
> Is this the story where the guy flies around
> on a kite that's being pulled by a boat and his
> shorts are down around his ankles?

> GK
> No, that's another story. This pontoon boat—

DUSTY
I thought it was a raft.

GK
It was a pontoon boat made to look like a
raft.

DUSTY
Oh. You said raft—

GK
It was a pontoon boat that they pretended
was a raft. Anyway, we hit the wake and she
tipped and the barbecue tipped over and red-
hot coals come skittering across the deck of
the boat and they all pitched themselves over
the rail—

LEFTY
What did that have to do with you going into
radio?

GK
I was just about to get to that.

DUSTY
This isn't the story about the kite?

GK
You know, when you keep interrupting . . .
you break the flow of a story.

LEFTY (TO DUSTY)
Yeah, shut up, let the man talk.

MOLLY
Mr. Keillor? Al is on the verge of a coronary
up there.

GK
Be right there.

He takes his pants off the hanger and steps into them.

10   INT. BACKSTAGE—SAME TIME

The door to the atrium is opened and YOLANDA JOHNSON
walks in, carrying two dresses on a hanger covered with
plastic and a small traveling suitcase, and behind her, each
holding dresses on hangers under clear plastic and traveling
bags, are YOLANDA's sister RHONDA and YOLANDA's
daughter LOLA.

YOLANDA
Thank you, Roberto.
Sorry we're late. There was a freight train.
Longest train I ever saw.

STAGEHAND 1
Hey, no problemo.

RHONDA
We left the car double-parked in the street—

STAGEHAND 1
I'll take care of it.

YOLANDA
You're a sweetheart.—Hi, John. Hi, Peter.

She walks by a little cluster of musicians jamming in the
corner, against the brick wall, and stops.

YOLANDA
That's the—what is that song?—that's . . .

RHONDA
"Honolulu Mama, could she dance, in her
pink pajamas when she took off her Oahu
Oahu Oahu . . ."

YOLANDA
Naw. It's a Carter Family song.

LOLA
A what?

YOLANDA
Carter Family, honey. Like us, except famous.

She walks into GUY NOIR's office. GUY NOIR is dozing in
his chair. She sets down her traveling bag and puts her arm
around LOLA, wanting her to look at the backstage scene, the
crowd, the lowered curtain, the heightened anticipation, and
remember it, memorize it.

YOLANDA
Look at this. Just look at it. I wish I had a
picture of it.

LOLA
So take one.

YOLANDA
This has been—home—since I was your age.
My mom used to drop us off at the door and
go home and listen to us sing on the radio.

LOLA
Fascinating.

GUY NOIR (O.C.)
Miss Yolanda and the luminous Lola.

RHONDA
Don't forget the resplendent Rhonda.

RHONDA vamps, flutters, as YOLANDA, grinning, reaches
for his hand.

YOLANDA
Mr. Noir—once more.

GUY NOIR
A pleasure.

GUY NOIR stands, takes YOLANDA's hand and bows. He
kisses LOLA's hand and kisses RHONDA on the cheek. He
picks up YOLANDA's traveling bag and takes the dress on the
hanger, and also the dress that LOLA is carrying, and tucks
her traveling bag under one arm, and leads them through the
backstage crowd.

GUY NOIR
I don't carry luggage in my line of work but I
make an exception for certain friends.

They turn across the stage in front of the Prairie Home house
and YOLANDA stops and touches the railing.

YOLANDA
Good-bye my old house. Good-bye porch.
We sat up here when we were kids,
remember?

RHONDA
Sat and shot rubber bands into the audience.
People thought they were fruit bats.

YOLANDA
What are they going to do with the house,
Guy?

GUY NOIR
They moved in a huge Dumpster yesterday.

(TO LOLA)
One of these gowns belong to you, *ma
cherie*?

With GUY NOIR leading the way, YOLANDA, LOLA, and
RHONDA make their way past the stage.

LOLA
Not really.

YOLANDA
Try it on. I'd just like to see it on you.

LOLA
I'd like to see it on *you*. It looks like
somebody's old bridesmaid dress. It's the
color of cat urine.

YOLANDA smiles a forced smile for the bystanders and then
stops, noticing a paper tacked to a bulletin board at the head
of the stairs. She reads it.

YOLANDA
What is this supposed to mean?

The notice on the bulletin board. In large black letters:

"ALL PERSONAL PROPERTY MUST BE REMOVED FROM
PREMISES IMMEDIATELY AFTER SHOW OR IT WILL BE
DESTROYED. NO EXCEPTIONS. MANAGEMENT."

YOLANDA (O.C.)
Who put this up here?

GUY NOIR
The boys upstairs, of course.

RHONDA (O.C.)
So it's true?

YOLANDA (O.C.)
I don't even want to think about it.

She looks at the notice, shudders, and heads down the stairs.

LOLA
What's the big deal?

YOLANDA
I can't talk about it.

MOLLY ON P.A. (O.C.)
Ladies and gentlemen—we are now eight
minutes from broadcast. Eight minutes.
Places, please.

STAGE MANAGER (O.C.)
Where'd Guy Noir go to? Hey, Noir! Noir!!!

10A INT. MAKEUP ROOM—SAME TIME

GK is pulling on his pants.

STAGE MANAGER ON P.A.
Guy Noir to the stage, please.

DONNA, the makeup lady, is spraying DUSTY's hair. LEFTY
shuffles the cards for another hand of solitaire.

DONNA
So how did you get into radio?

GK

One of those guys who fell off the raft was
Old Man Soderberg and he couldn't swim
and I got him to shore.

DUSTY
So you saved his life.

GK

Well, the water was fairly shallow but he
didn't know that because I was towing him
pretty fast.

LEFTY
And he gave you a job here at WLT.

GK
His brother did.

DONNA
Art Soderberg.

GK
Right. The one on the raft was Ray
Soderberg.

LEFTY
So Art Soderberg gave you the job—

DONNA
It was on the early-morning show.

LEFTY
Dusty and I used to have an early-morning
show.

DUSTY

Breakfast in the Bunkhouse . . . TV show. We
showed cartoons.

GK

It was a show called *The Rise and Shine Show,*
with a guy named Wilmer Scott.

DONNA

Came on at five o'clock in the morning.
Gospel show.

GK

Right. Inspirational show.

LEFTY

Wasn't Wilmer Scott a famous aviator?

GK

You're thinking of Wilbur Scott.

LEFTY

First man to fly solo the length of the
Mississippi River.

GK

Wilbur Scott.

LEFTY

Flew from New Orleans to Memphis to
Minnesota all the way to Lake Itasca and
celebrated his success by firing a signal
rocket out the cockpit window and became
the first civilian pilot to shoot himself down.

DUSTY

You made that up.

LEFTY
Crashed in the lake at his moment of
triumph.

GK
Anyway, this was his brother Wilmer Scott.

DONNA
The Rise and Shine Show . . .

GK
He'd been doing the show for thirty years
and the only way he could form words and
sentences at 5 AM—

MOLLY enters, breathless.

MOLLY
Really—we need you upstairs—okay?

GK
Be right there. —The only way he could talk
at 5 AM—

DONNA
—was to pour himself a little eye-opener—

MOLLY
Al is about to self-destruct—

DONNA
—and by the time GK was hired, the old
bugger was pouring himself about five or six
eye-openers—

MOLLY
He is stripping his gears.

GK

I'll be right up. Just as soon as she finishes
telling my story.

DUSTY

Lefty and me never drank. We learned how
to take little naps sitting up with our eyes
open.

DONNA

GK's first day on the job, old Wilmer went on
the air and told eight or ten dirty limericks—

LEFTY

On the air?

GK

On the air.

DUSTY

I think I remember hearing that. I was a small
child—

MOLLY

I am going to lose my job if you don't come.
Think about the baby!

She grimaces and ducks out.

11   INT. BACKSTAGE—CONTINUOUS

GUY NOIR sits at the stage-door security desk, pouring
powdered creamer into a cup of coffee and stirring it.

GUY NOIR

I was helping her with her luggage.

STAGE MANAGER (O.C.)
You're supposed to be guarding the door.

GUY NOIR reaches into a desk drawer and pulls out a silver
flask and unscrews the cap and pours liquid into the coffee to
the very rim of the cup, stops, leans down, and sips from the
cup where it sits on the desk so as not to waste a drop.

GUY NOIR
What you worried about?

STAGE MANAGER (O.C.)
We had some weird call from a crazy lady.

GUY NOIR rummages in the desk drawer and comes up with
a ruler, a pair of pliers, a length of electric cord, a paperback, a
bobblehead, a cell phone, various flotsam, before finding what
he wants: a pack of matches. From his breast pocket, he pulls
out a cigar, puts it in his mouth, and lights it.

GUY NOIR
She ain't that crazy.

STAGE MANAGER (O.C.)
How do you know?

GUY NOIR
She came in this afternoon.

STAGE MANAGER (O.C.)
You get a description?

GUY NOIR
She was beautiful. Her hair was what God
had in mind when he said, "Let there be hair."

GUY NOIR stands, walks toward the camera.

GUY NOIR
She gave me a smile so sweet you coulda
poured it on your pancakes.

The camera pulls back as GUY NOIR stops and leans forward
to whisper into the STAGE MANAGER's ear.

GUY NOIR
Her jeans were so tight I could read the label
on her underwear. It said, "Tuesday. Wash in
lukewarm water and spin lightly."

STAGE MANAGER
You're making it up.

GUY NOIR
She was wearing a Mount Rushmore T-shirt
and I never saw those guys look so good.
Especially Jefferson and Lincoln. It was an
honor to sit and inhale the same air that she
had so recently exhaled . . . just to . . . exchange
the atmosphere between us. So to speak.

STAGE MANAGER
What'd she want?

GUY NOIR
She had the wrong address. She was looking
for the Presbyterian church. And like a dope I
told her where it was . . . and away she went.
Gone.

He looks to his left and does a double take at MOLLY,
standing there.

GUY NOIR
I didn't know you were pregnant. My God.
When did this take place?

MOLLY
Guy—buddy—pal—

GUY NOIR
Who did this to you, honey?

He slips a protective arm around her.

MOLLY
For a detective, there's a lot you don't detect.

GUY NOIR
Who was it?

MOLLY
I don't mean this in a critical way, but the
word *clueless* comes to mind.

DUSTY and LEFTY, passing by, stop.

GUY NOIR
Tell me it wasn't anybody from around the
show.

MOLLY
It wasn't anybody from around the show.

GUY NOIR
That's good.

(TO DUSTY & LEFTY)
Our little girl is going to be a single mother.

LEFTY
You poor thing.

DUSTY
It wasn't me, darling! I swear on the Bible.

LEFTY (SINGS)
"Do not scorn her with words fierce and bitter
Do not laugh at her shame and downfall."

DUSTY & LEFTY (SING)
"For a moment just stop and consider
That a man was the cause of it all."

STAGE MANAGER (O.C.)
Dusty!

DUSTY
Yo!

STAGE MANAGER (O.C.)
About that obscene song you sang on the
show last week—

DUSTY
What song?

STAGE MANAGER (O.C.)
"Come ride my pony, all the night long.
Come ride him bareback and I'll sing you a song."

That one.

DUSTY
It was about riding a pony.

GUY NOIR
Right.

DUSTY
What did you think it was about?

STAGE MANAGER
Let's go out with a little class, okay? What do
you say?

DUSTY
"Go out"? What are you talking about?

STAGE MANAGER
Just what I said.

DUSTY
"Go out"? You mean me?

GUY NOIR
All of us.

DUSTY
What in the Sam Hill are you talking about?

The LUNCH LADY approaches with a cardboard box lined
with plastic and full of sandwiches wrapped in waxed paper.

LUNCH LADY
Got some nice egg salad sandwiches if you're
hungry.

MOLLY
I'm always hungry.

GUY NOIR (TO LUNCH LADY)
Did you know Molly is pregnant? Ain't that
something?

DUSTY (TO LUNCH LADY)
How about a leg sandwich?

(HE GROWLS SEDUCTIVELY)
Huh? Want me to show you how that goes?

He drapes an arm over the LUNCH LADY's shoulder and she pushes him away, playfully.

LUNCH LADY
Don't you ever think of anything else?

DUSTY
I think about it so if I should meet a woman
who's thinking about it, too, then there'd be
two of us, Lillian.

LUNCH LADY
Evelyn.

DUSTY
Evelyn! Your sister was Lillian.

LUNCH LADY
I don't have a sister.

CUT TO:

12   INT. MAKEUP ROOM—SAME TIME

GK is lacing up his shoes. DONNA is spiffing up CHUCK AKERS and trying to do something with his hair as he stands, restless, at the makeup table.

GK
He did "There was a young fellow from
Buckingham" and the bishop of Chichester
and the young man from Antietam and the
old man of Khartoum who kept a young
sheep in his room and "A young woman got
on her knees and said to her lover, 'Oh
please, it will heighten my bliss if you do
more with this and pay less attention to
these.'"

CHUCK AKERS
I'm going to remember that one and tell it to
Evie.

DONNA
What happened to Wilmer Scott?

GK
Nothing.

DONNA
He didn't get fired?

GK
Nope.

CHUCK AKERS
I thought you got into radio when he got
fired—

GK
People couldn't believe that that beloved old
man would stoop so low so they decided
they hadn't heard it.

CHUCK AKERS
Bless their hearts.

STAGE MANAGER ON P.A.
Two minutes to broadcast, people. I mean it.
This is not a test. This is an actual warning.

MOLLY enters, out of breath.

MOLLY
Please. Come. Now.

MOLLY grabs on to the wall and sags. Her eyes get big. She pants. She starts to slide down the wall toward a squatting position.

> MOLLY
> I am going into labor. I just got a contraction the size of Vermont. Oh my gosh. Oh my God. It's coming. I'm about to have my baby right here on this filthy floor. Call me an ambulance.

> CHUCK AKERS (O.C.)
> Okay, you're an ambulance.

MOLLY looks up and smiles.

> MOLLY
> Never mind. False alarm.

There is a chorus of good-humored protest and MOLLY, GK, and CHUCK AKERS head out the makeup room door and up the steep stairs to the stage.

13   INT. STAIRS TO THE STAGE—CONTINUOUS

> GK
> Wilmer Scott came on the show ten years ago and hypnotized chickens. Remember that?

> CHUCK AKERS
> Sure do. Hypnotized four chickens right in a row.

> MOLLY
> Who was Wilmer Scott?

CHUCK AKERS
He ran his finger down their foreheads
between their eyes and he says, "Cheese
chips, parsnips, and charlie" until the bird's
eyes were crossed and he set it down and did
the next one. Did four in a row.

MOLLY
Who was Wilmer Scott?

GK
He used to do the *Rise and Shine Show*—

CHUCK AKERS
That's where GK started out in radio—

MOLLY
And he hypnotized chickens?

14   INT. FITZGERALD WINGS—CONTINUOUS

The three of them have reached the stage left wings where
musicians sit along the rope rail. They head for the stage—the
curtain is still down—and pass the mixing board where it
stands, in the wings but extending partly onstage, with racks
of electronic gear behind it. The TECHNICAL DIRECTOR and
HIS ASSISTANT stand at the board, an old multichannel
mixer with two small monitor speakers mounted on it, and
lighted dials and meters. The equipment is battered and
outdated, a jerry-built assemblage of odd parts, cordage on the
floor. A large trophy stands on the front rim of the board.

GK
Not on that show. This show. Hypnotized
four or five chickens.

(TO TECHNICAL DIRECTOR)
You remember those chickens that guy
hypnotized, don't you?

TECHNICAL DIRECTOR
Oh yeah.

GK, MOLLY, and CHUCK AKERS stop by the mixing board.

MOLLY
Why would you hypnotize chickens on the
radio where nobody could see it?

CHUCK AKERS
People just liked the idea of it, I guess.

MOLLY
But how did they know the chickens were
hypnotized?

TECHNICAL DIRECTOR
It got real quiet.

MOLLY
Al is waving at us over there.

GK
They were beautiful brown chickens with
those sort of leggings around their ankles.

TECHNICAL DIRECTOR
They were Chinese chickens.

MOLLY
The curtain is about to come up.

CHUCK AKERS
One of the chickens flew out into the
audience.

GK
Landed in a lady's lap. The wife of a sponsor.

CHUCK AKERS
She let out a screech, it sounded like the
orphanage was on fire. I'll never forget it.

He reaches over to the mixing board and picks up the trophy.
It's a pedestal with columns and goddesses and a golden
wreath and lyre.

CHUCK AKERS
That is the ugliest damn trophy I ever saw.
Who's that for?

MOLLY
It's for the Employee of the Month.

CHUCK AKERS
Looks like something they'd tie to your ankle
when they throw you overboard to make
sure you stay under.

MOLLY
So did you get to how you got into radio?

CHUCK AKERS
He was just about to.

He turns away.

GK (TO MOLLY)
This *Rise and Shine Show* that came
on at 5 AM was sponsored by
Piscacadawadaquoddymoggin medicinal
tonic.

GK and MOLLY head out onstage where the SHOE BAND
and ROBIN and LINDA are tuning, getting set for the show. A
STAGEHAND is checking the curtain to make sure it's clear of
the mic stands and stage monitors.

MOLLY
Pisca what?

GK
Piscacadawadaquoddymoggin, made from
sassafras, buffalo grass, and pure grain
alcohol.

MOLLY
You advertised that on the radio?

GK
It was what Wilmer Scott drank in his coffee
before he went on the air—

MOLLY
What was it called?

ROBIN
Piscacadawadaquoddymoggin Medicinal
Home Formula.

GK
No, it's Piscacadawadaquoddymoggin.

ROBIN
That's what I said.

STAGE MANAGER (O.C.)
Places. Thirty seconds.

MOLLY steps back and gives GK the once-over.

MOLLY
Check your barn door.

GK stops momentarily to zip.

GK
Anyway, Wilmer Scott used to have a
snootful every morning and then he just
upped and quit.

ROBIN
How'd he do that?

STAGE MANAGER (O.C.)
Quiet onstage!

GK
He just did it.
Remember the jingle—

ROBIN & LINDA & GK (SING)
Piscacadawadaquoddymoggin
medicinal formula.

GK (TO MOLLY)
He quit drinking and suddenly he developed
mic fright and he went into the chicken
business.

MOLLY
Chinese chickens—

GK
Show chickens. Lot of money in that.

The curtain rises.

MOLLY
You're on.

GK (SINGS)
O hear that old piano from down the avenue,
I smell the pine trees, I look around for you.
My sweet old someone, coming through that door,
It's Saturday and the band is playing,
Honey, could we ask for more.

The camera pulls back. In the wings, watching, are CHUCK
AKERS and the LUNCH LADY. His arm is around her.

CHUCK AKERS
I'm gonna play that song for you today,
darling.

LUNCH LADY (SHE GIGGLES)
You're not going to dedicate it to me, are
you?

CHUCK AKERS
In my heart I will.

CUT TO:

15   INT. DRESSING ROOM

RHONDA is holding up a gown, looking at herself in the
mirror. There are photographs of family in gold frames on the
dressing room table, makeup utensils laid out. One easy chair
and a couple of folding chairs. A sink. Some show posters on

the walls. YOLANDA sits at the table, doing her nails. LOLA
sits in the easy chair, staring at the back of YOLANDA's head,
writing on a pad of paper.

> GK (O.C.)
> Hello everybody and welcome to *A Prairie
> Home Companion* . . . coming to you live on a
> Saturday night from the Fitzgerald Theater in
> downtown St. Paul and brought to you as
> always by Powdermilk Biscuits . . . heavens
> they're tasty and expeditious . . . by the
> Ketchup Advisory Board, ketchup with
> natural mellowing agents—

> LOLA
> Turn it down.

RHONDA reaches up and turns down the volume knob.

> RHONDA
> I'm going to color my hair strawberry
> blonde. I swear to God I should've done it
> years ago.

She gives herself a good long look in the mirror.

> RHONDA (CONT'D)
> I should've broke loose and gone to Chicago
> back when Mama died, that's when I
> should've done it. You put those things off
> and you never get around to it again.

> YOLANDA (TO LOLA)
> Thank you for coming, sweetheart. I hope
> you know how much it means to me.

LOLA looks up blankly from her writing.

YOLANDA
I just want you to be here. Our last show.
Remember when you came as a kid?

RHONDA
You were just a sprite.

LOLA
I remember that guy with the bad breath.

RHONDA
You wore your little sailor getup with those
doodads in your hair.

LOLA
I remember he coughed—it would've
knocked a buzzard off a manure spreader.

YOLANDA
I'm so excited you're going to sing something
with us.

LOLA rolls her eyes.

LOLA
I said maybe.

She resumes writing.

YOLANDA
I hope I don't have a stroke. . . . What are you
writing?

LOLA
A poem.

YOLANDA
A poem about what?

LOLA
Suicide.

YOLANDA
Oh. Okay.

15A INT. FITZGERALD STAGE—SAME TIME

GK
Are you tired of your current herring? Has it
lost that certain something you look for in a
pickled fish product?
Then maybe it's time you try Jens Jensen—
the Lake Superior herring made the old
Norwegian way.

(HE SINGS, TO TUNE OF "WON'T YOU COME HOME, BILL
BAILEY")
Vil du komm hjem, Jens Jensen
Vil du komm hjem?
Hos Svend og Nils og Karen.
Jeg vil vaske op, min elske,
Betale hus leje,
And give you lots of herring.
Jeg huske den regnfuld aften
Jeg smed dig ud,
Du vandrede til ost og vest.
Det er min skam,
Det er min skyld.
Jens Jensen herring is the best.

Jens Jensen . . . ask for it by name, and if your
grocer doesn't stock it, ask him why not. Jens
Jensen . . . spelled with a J, pronounced like a
Y. Why? Because it yust is.

RHONDA reaches into her purse on the table and pulls out a bottle of whiskey and pours some into a paper cup. She sits on the table, raises the cup.

> RHONDA
> I don't think I care to do "Softly and Tenderly Jesus Is Calling" tonight, okay?

She tosses back the whiskey and shudders dramatically, shaking her cheeks, vocalizing.

> RHONDA
> Boy, that's good stuff. Here we are. A lush, a stroke victim, and a suicidal teenager.

> YOLANDA
> You know what my philosophy is?

> LOLA
> Yes, I do, so don't tell me.

> YOLANDA
> I think you've got to be grateful for every-thing that happens to you because that's what got you here, and if you hadn't gone through whatever you went through, you wouldn't have wound up where you are right now. So disappointment doesn't get you anywhere.

> RHONDA
> Well, aren't you wonderful.

> YOLANDA
> One door closes and another one opens. Everything is a step along the way and it leads to something else. You just take it as it comes.

She rises and walks to LOLA and stands over her.

> YOLANDA
> Read me some of your poem.

> LOLA (READING)
> "Soliloquy for a Blue Guitar."

Death is easy like jumping into the big
blue air and waving hello to god
god is love but
he doesn't necessarily drop everything and
catch you does he
So when you hook the hose up to your tailpipe,
Don't expect to wake up and get toast for breakfast.
The toast is you.

YOLANDA lets a long silent moment pass.

> LOLA
> Like it?

> YOLANDA (TO RHONDA)
> You remember that song we sang with
> Rusty?

> (TO LOLA)
> We used to have a dog in the act when
> Connie and Wanda were in it and we'd sing
> this song with him and he'd howl.

> YOLANDA & RHONDA (SING)
> Go tell Aunt Gladys
> Go tell Aunt Gladys
> Go tell Aunt Gladys
> Her old brown dog is dead.

YOLANDA & RHONDA (SING) (CONT'D)
An old brown dog named Rusty
An old brown dog named Rusty
An old brown dog named Rusty
He just laid down and died.

They howl in two-part harmony.

YOLANDA & RHONDA (SING)
He died from chasing squirrels
He died from chasing squirrels
He died from chasing squirrels
He ate one and got sick.

It must've been a bad one
It must've been a bad one
It must've been a bad one
He just lay down and died.

They howl in harmony.

LOLA
You sang that in public?

RHONDA
That was the summer we auditioned for the
Lawrence Welk Show and Mama made those
big yellow dresses with the puff sleeves and
the petticoats.

YOLANDA
We went to Hollywood on the train and we
promised Mama that we would lock
ourselves into our hotel rooms and not walk
the streets—

LOLA
At night?

YOLANDA

Anytime. And we promised we were going
to sing "Softly and Tenderly Jesus Is Calling,
Calling for You and for Me"—

RHONDA

And we would have, except that "Softly and
Tenderly Jesus Is Calling" just didn't show
us off to advantage. It wasn't going to get us
the job.

YOLANDA

So we did our bird medley instead.

LOLA

You never told me about this.

RHONDA

It was absolutely terrific. "When the Red Red
Robin Comes Bob Bob Bobbin Along," which
segued into "His Eye Is on the Sparrow" and
"Bluebird of Happiness" and then "Bye Bye
Blackbird." The audience went nuts. They
were standing, clapping, waving hankies,
throwing babies in the air. And you know
something? They cut that number out of the
show. You want to know why? Envy. Pure
and simple. They could not bear to see four
little girls from Oshkosh, Wisconsin, tear up
an audience like that and show up the
Lennon Sisters. So all they left in was "Go
Tell Aunt Gladys the Old Brown Dog Is
Dead," which we did as an encore. It was
pure envy. The Lennon Sisters. We could sing
circles around the Lennon Sisters. So they
dumped us. The Lennon Sisters were
communists. It's true. That is not generally
known.

(TO YOLANDA)
Don't look at me like that. It's true. We had
more talent in our little pinkie than the four
of them put together. They hated us because
we were better than they were.

YOLANDA
Mr. Welk was nice.

RHONDA
We didn't know it at the time but that was
the high point of our career. Only time we got
to Hollywood. I was thirteen, you were ten,
Wanda was, what?

YOLANDA
Sixteen. And Connie was fifteen.

RHONDA
That was it. End of the road. Envy.

YOLANDA
Anyway, Wanda took it hard, and a week
later, she got arrested.

LOLA
For what? You never told me about this.

YOLANDA
Shoplifting.

RHONDA
She was in a café having a cup of coffee and
she ordered a glazed doughnut and started
eating it and got a sugar rush and jumped
up, forgetting that she hadn't paid for it and
she walked out the door . . . and two minutes
later there were red lights flashing and she

RHONDA (CONT'D)
was in handcuffs and the TV cameras were
there and she was bawling and her hair was a
mess and it was on the ten o'clock newscast
and Daddy saw it—

YOLANDA
He was in the hospital with Mama who was
having her tubes tied after Johnny was born.

RHONDA
Daddy saw Wanda on TV getting arrested for
shoplifting and he had a major coronary
occlusion.

LOLA
That was when he died?

RHONDA
It was fatal, yes.

YOLANDA
He just pulled the sheet up over his own face,
and when the nurse came in, he was dead.

RHONDA
He left a note for Wanda. She was released
from jail for the funeral. The note said, "You
broke my heart." Signed, Daddy.

YOLANDA
She did thirty days in jail for one glazed
doughnut.

LOLA
That's terrible.

RHONDA
Fifty-nine-cent doughnut.

RHONDA is putting on her eyelashes.

RHONDA
If it was rock 'n' roll, she could've thrown
sofas out of the hotel window, but when
you're working to Christian family audiences
like we were, if you so much as forget to pay
for a doughnut, they'll dump you like you
were a piece of garbage.

YOLANDA
She quit the act and joined the Sisters of
Perpetual Sorrow and went off to live in a
convent in Minot where you spend eight
hours a day on your knees rocking back and
forth and moaning.

RHONDA
One week we're in Hollywood on the verge
of stardom and a week later we're back
playing the county fair circuit and doing our
costume changes in the ladies' toilet and boys
trying to peek in and then you go and sing
outdoors with a cloud of mosquitoes around
your head . . . I remember that time when a
dragonfly came right in my mouth, almost
choked me—I thought I'd swallowed a bird.

YOLANDA
It was "I'll Fly Away." She finished the rest of
the verse and then she turned around to spit
during the instrumental.

LOLA is moved by this tale of sorrow and disappointment,
her eyes are teary.

LOLA
What happened to your mother?

RHONDA
Your grandma lost her marbles when Daddy
expired. She always had been wound sort of
tight and she went off the deep end and she
started cleaning her house more or less
twenty-four hours a day.

YOLANDA
The neighbors could hear her vacuum
cleaner at three and four in the morning. It
was obsessive-compulsive. She vacuumed
the hell out of that carpet. Vacuumed it right
down to bare threads.

RHONDA
We had to shovel her into the Good Shepherd
Home. And Connie left the act to stay and
take care of Mama and then there were just
the two of us. And your dad—he was the one
who got us on the radio. Before he ran off
with the yodeler. Your mom's best friend.
Ardelle.

LOLA
She could yodel?

RHONDA
When she met him she could. And then he
just gradually wore the yodeling out of her.
She sang at Mama's funeral. We couldn't. We
were basket cases. So your dad and Ardelle
sang.

LOLA
What did they sing at the funeral?

YOLANDA (SINGS)
Softly and tenderly Jesus is calling
Calling for you and for me,
See on the portals he's waiting and watching,
Watching for you and for me.

YOLANDA & RHONDA (SING)
Come home, come home,
Ye who are weary come home—

RHONDA
And that night your dad ran off with Ardelle
and they drove to Bakersfield, California.

LOLA
My father ran off with my mother's best
friend after singing a hymn at Grandma's
funeral? Jesus.

YOLANDA
You were two years old. And you know
something? I didn't care about him so long as
I had you. That's the truth.

16   INT. HALLWAY OUTSIDE THE DRESSING ROOM—SAME
TIME

GK knocks on the door with "JOHNSON SISTERS" written on it.

The door opens. RHONDA is there. Inside, YOLANDA and
LOLA are singing.

YOLANDA & LOLA
Come home, come home
Ye who are weary come home—

RHONDA
Are we on?

GK
Got a few minutes.

MOLLY stands behind him.

YOLANDA
What are we doing?

MOLLY
You're on in the Powdermilk segment doing
"Gold Watch & Chain"—with him—

YOLANDA
Haven't done that for years.

(SHE SINGS)
I will pawn you my gold watch and chain, love

(GK JOINS)
I will pawn you my gold wedding ring
I will pawn you this heart in my bosom
If you only will love me again.

RHONDA (TO GK)
I'm getting a head start on getting pie-eyed.

YOLANDA
How about "Red River Valley"?

GK
Whatever you want.

YOLANDA takes a look in the mirror, dabs at her eyeliner
with a tissue.

YOLANDA
I want to make sure there's a spot for Lola
later—

GK
I saw her name on the order.

LOLA
Is this really the last show?

GK
Every show is the last show. That's my
philosophy.

RHONDA
Thank you, Plato.

He leaves as JEARLYN STEELE enters, an African American
woman in a golden dress, hair done up high on her head.

JEARLYN
Hi, everybody.

YOLANDA
Jearlyn!

(TO LOLA)
Jearlyn used to babysit you, remember?

(TO JEARLYN)
You look fantastic.

JEARLYN
When you're this big, honey, you gotta look
fantastic, there is no way around it. I was
going to say good-bye, but I'm afraid I'm
gonna start crying, so I won't.

YOLANDA
Good. Let's not.

MOLLY
Let's go, everybody.

YOLANDA
Lola's going to sing tonight.

JEARLYN
Hey. Sing something with me, baby.

She turns to see LOLA looking at herself in the mirror, holding up in front of her a show dress like her mother's.

LOLA
Do you think I'm attractive?

CUT TO:

16A INT. MAKEUP ROOM

The LUNCH LADY stands behind DUSTY who is sitting on a chair. She is kneading his shoulders.

DUSTY
A little to the left. Oh, God, that's good.
Down a little. Mmmmmmm.

LUNCH LADY
I should be getting back upstairs. I told Lola
I'd make her a turkey sandwich.

DUSTY
Don't stop yet. You're driving me wild.
You're a good back rubber.

(HE SINGS)
I used to work in Chicago
At a department store
I used to work in Chicago
I did but I don't anymore.
A lady came in for a girdle,
I asked her what kind she wore.
"Rubber," she said, and rub her I did
And I don't work there anymore.

LUNCH LADY
This is our last show. I can't believe it. I've
been working here twenty-five years. What's
going to happen to me?

DUSTY (SINGS)
I used to work in Chicago
At a department store
I used to work in Chicago
I did but I don't anymore.
A lady came in for a birthday cake,
I asked her what kind and what for.
"Layer," she said, and lay her I did
And I don't work there anymore.

17   INT. FITZGERALD THEATER—SAME TIME

Onstage, the band is switching over, musicians coming and
going, stagehands moving microphones. GK at the podium.

GK
—and right now let's bring up an old favorite
here on *A Prairie Home Companion* and that's a
couple of fine ladies who've been singing
together since they were little girls in
Oshkosh, Wisconsin.

CUT TO:

RHONDA and YOLANDA slip through the crowd in the
wings toward the stage.

> GK (O.C.)
> They've kept alive all the wonderful old
> songs that have been around forever, and
> they've been like sisters to all of us, and let's
> all welcome *the Johnson Girls.*

RHONDA sticks her tongue out at GK as she passes upstage of
him and she and YOLANDA come to the front of the stage.
YOLANDA waves to the audience.

> GK (CONT'D)
> Yolanda and Rhonda, it wouldn't be a show
> without you.

> YOLANDA
> Thank you so much. Thank you.

RHONDA is gesturing to the audience for more applause.
YOLANDA gestures for her to stop.

> YOLANDA
> I just want to say how happy I am that my
> daughter Lola came tonight.

> (SHE GLANCES TOWARD THE WINGS)
> Thank you, sweetheart. It means a lot to me. I
> named my little girl after my mother, Lola.
> And now we'd like to do an old song that
> Mama loved—she was our inspiration, you
> know. Nobody worked harder than our
> mama—washing and cleaning and cooking
> and looking after six kids—and the main
> reason we wanted to make music was that it

YOLANDA (CONT'D)
was the only way we knew to make Mama
happy. She'd be on her knees scrubbing the
kitchen floor and if you stood in the doorway
and sang a song she liked, she'd look up and
smile, worn-out as she was, and you could
see her gold tooth.

Behind her, RHONDA is counting off the tempo to the band.

RHONDA (TO BAND ONSTAGE)
Not too fast—

(COUNTING OFF TIME, SNAPPING FINGERS)
—or I'll kill you sons of bitches, and I
mean it.

She turns and smiles to the audience, as band plays.

YOLANDA & RHONDA (SING)
Way down upon that old Mississippi River,
Not so far away
That's where my folks have lived forever,
That's where I'm going to stay.
I've been looking cross the whole creation
Half my life and more.
And then I found my sweet satisfaction
Right here on the muddy river shore.

CUT TO:

19 INT. BACKSTAGE—SAME TIME

The backstage crowd turning its attention toward the stage,
musicians, stagehands, the STAGE MANAGER on the phone,
MOLLY, GK, and then LOLA joins them. DUSTY is behind her.

JOHNSON GIRLS (V.O.)
All of the world, it is so sad and weary,
Everywhere I roam.
Oh Mama, how I missed the prairie,
And my Minnesota home.

CUT TO:

20   INT. STAGE—SAME TIME

YOLANDA JOHNSON onstage.

YOLANDA (SINGS)
I can see Mama on Sunday mornings
All the good old hymns that were sung
We knelt in prayer with our aunts and uncles,
Who loved us when we were young.
In the valley of darkness, they are the shepherds
Who lead me to the pastures green
And I'll sit with mama by the still still waters,
And goodness and mercy follow me.

21   INT. FITZGERALD WINGS—SAME TIME

Beyond the crowd in the wings, GUY NOIR stands at the
security desk, staring into the camera.

JOHNSON GIRLS (SING O.C.)
I've floated down the Columbia and the Hudson
Walked on the banks of the O-hi-o.

GUY NOIR
You came back.

DANGEROUS WOMAN (O.C.)
I did.

GUY NOIR

The Presbyterians weren't what you were
looking for?

JOHNSON GIRLS (SING O.C.)

On the banks of the Wabash and the mighty Colorado
And the old Red River way up north.

DANGEROUS WOMAN (O.C.)

No. I was sent here, Mr. Noir.

GUY NOIR

What can I do for you?

DANGEROUS WOMAN (O.C.)

Really nothing, Mr. Noir. I'll take care of it.
You have a nice show here.

JOHNSON GIRLS (SING O.C.)

All the world it is a world of rivers
Flowing to the sea
Here along the dear Mississippi
Here is the home for you and me.

LOLA stands in the wings, watching. DUSTY and LEFTY
stand behind her. GUY NOIR, beyond them, is staring ahead.
He is stunned by the presence of the woman.

GUY NOIR

Thanks. We like it.

DANGEROUS WOMAN (O.C.)

Do you believe in the fullness of time and the
spirit? Most people don't, you know. But it
would be good, Mr. Noir, if you opened your
heart to the fullness of time—and to the spirit

(SHE GENUFLECTS)
which upholds and sustains us all through
this world. Amen.

GUY NOIR
Whatever you say.

He gazes at her as the DANGEROUS WOMAN, in a white
raincoat, a Twins baseball cap, and dark glasses, puts her hand
on his shoulder and moves past him to stand behind LOLA.

CUT TO:

22   INT. FITZGERALD STAGE—SAME TIME

The JOHNSON GIRLS hold hands, singing, as musicians come
onstage behind them for the next act.

JOHNSON GIRLS (SINGING)
All of the world, it is so sad and weary,
Everywhere I roam.
Oh Mama, how I missed the prairie,
And my Minnesota home.

Audience applause. GK looks up and grins and gestures to his
right.

GK
The Johnson Girls . . . thank you. Brought to
you by Powdermilk Biscuits . . . heavens,
they're tasty and expeditious, made from
whole wheat raised by Norwegian bachelor
farmers so you know they're good for you
and pure mostly . . . and by Jack's Auto
Repair, where the bright flashing lights show
you the way to complete satisfaction.

GK (CONT'D)
I'd like to come in and sing a song and send
this out to all the friends in my hometown.

(HE SINGS)
Slow days of summer in this old town
Sun goes across the sky
Sometimes a car goes by
There's one right now.

Looks like a Chevy. Your Chev is blue.
This Chev is white and brown
It isn't slowing down,
Guess it's not you.

(As he sings, DANGEROUS WOMAN appears in the doorway
of the Prairie Home set upstage from him.)

You said you'd be here Sunday or so.
Maybe by Saturday,
If you could get away,
You didn't know.

I love you darling, waiting alone.
Waiting for you to show.
Wishing you'd call me though
I don't have a phone.

(DANGEROUS WOMAN emerges from the set and stands on
the porch, watching him.)

Waiting for love to come, all comes alive.
Birds sing in angel tongues
Small stones like diamonds
All down the drive.

(HE SINGS) (CONT'D)
Visions of love appear, clouds passing through
All of my life, I see
Passing so beautifully
Waiting for you.

(GUY NOIR appears in the doorway of Prairie Home, in
pursuit of DANGEROUS WOMAN as she crosses the stage.)

> Around the corner, an old dog appears
> Stands in the summer sun
> Waiting for love to come.
> Wish you were here.

GK
Prince of Pizza, the frozen pizza that tastes
homemade. With real Minnesota mozzarella
and sausage.

(HE SINGS, TO TUNE OF "LA DONNA E MOBILE")

> One Prince of Pizza slice
> Puts me in paradise,
> Sausage and extra cheese
> Onions and anchovies,
> You can stay home
> And feel you're in Rome
> No need to go ta
> Italy, you can eat prettily here in Minnesota.

Prince of Pizza.

CUT TO:

The camera follows GK past the STAGE MANAGER and into
the wings, through the crowd of musicians. Then we see the
LUNCH LADY holding her box of sandwiches up to the
DANGEROUS WOMAN.

LUNCH LADY
Egg salad or ham salad?

DANGEROUS WOMAN
Why are you crying?

LUNCH LADY
It's the last show. I'm never going to see these
people again.

DANGEROUS WOMAN
You'll see them again.

LUNCH LADY
Chuck and I . . . been dating for years. I can't
believe this is the last show.

(SHE WEEPS)
All of them from the old days—Soupy
Schindler, Red Maddock, Ray Marklund,
Helen Schneyer—gone and forgotten.

DANGEROUS WOMAN
Every sparrow is remembered.

LUNCH LADY
I don't even know as they're going to make a
speech or anything. . . . It doesn't seem right,
does it? Some big company come in and step
on us like we were bugs at the picnic?

LEFTY sits in one of the makeup chairs as DONNA powders his face. CHUCK AKERS lounges nearby, enjoying a beer and a smoke. GUY NOIR sits on the counter, examining his nails. The YODELER sits on a folding chair. She is a stocky woman in a cowgirl suit, her hair stiff with hairspray, heavily made up. GK voice, reading a commercial, comes from the monitor speaker on the wall. GUY NOIR reaches up and turns it off.

                    DONNA
          So when are we going to tell the people that
          this is the end? That it's the last show? Why
          the big silence? I don't get it.

GUY NOIR leans up close to the mirror and examines his eyebrows and his nostrils for nose hair.

                    GUY NOIR
               Maybe it's not.

                    CHUCK AKERS
          It's my last, that's for sure. Old lady laid
          down the law—

                    DONNA
          Don't kid yourself. You know it as well as I
          do. Plain as the nose on your face. They sold
          us down the river.

                    CHUCK AKERS
          Put her foot down. Told me she was going to
          hitch up the trailer, head south.

                    LEFTY
          Trim the eyebrows, wouldja? Thanks.

GUY NOIR
Maybe they're trying to spook us.

DONNA
The Soderberg family selling out . . . I just
don't get it. They've owned WLT since they
ran it out of the sandwich shop. That's what
the call letters stand for. With Lettuce and
Tomato. How can you just walk away from
something like that? What are we, used
Kleenex?

GUY NOIR
They got old, babes. They started to think
about ease and comfort. They saw a brochure
for an island with palm trees and an azure
sky and miles of sand and they said, "Hey,
what are we suffering through these winters
for? We don't have to freeze our butts waiting
for the bus to come—our bus has come! It's
here! We'll leave the business to the kids and
head for paradise and to hell with it."
Problem is, the kids had gone down to
paradise ahead of them. So there was this big
corporation in Texas that offered them a
gazillion dollars for it and, okay, maybe they
did talk funny and their eyes didn't focus and
their flesh was rotting and falling off, but hey,
nobody's perfect, and money is money, so the
Soderbergs took the dough. End of story.

DONNA
You'd think one of them would have the
decency to come down here and tell us in
person. Look us in the eye and tell us—

LEFTY
Don't take too much off the eyebrows—

CHUCK AKERS
I played at Chad Soderberg's wedding
reception at the Minnesota Club. It was nice.
Had a smoked salmon the size of a golden
retriever.

LEFTY
I remember that.

CHUCK AKERS
Were you there?

LEFTY
We were wearing tuxedos, remember?

DONNA
What are we supposed to do, just walk off
the cliff?

GUY NOIR
I wasn't going to tell you this, but . . .
between you and me and the flies on the
wall, there's a woman on the premises who I
think maybe is going to save our bacon. She's
got that look about her.

DONNA
Who is she?

GUY NOIR
I'm still working on figuring that out.

DONNA (TO LEFTY)
Close your eyes. Is she from NorComm?

GUY NOIR

Could be. Time will tell. I'll just let personal
charm do its work. She walked in—couldn't
take her eyes off me. Drawn to me like a
moth to the flame.

LEFTY

Maybe she needs a firm hand. The old
cowboy touch.

GUY NOIR

She asked about you, but I had to tell her
about your problem. All those years in the
saddle . . . alas, it took the lead right out of
your pencil. But I told her you know quite a
lot about fabrics and home decor, should she
need a decorator.

YODELER (TO DONNA)

You going to be able to get to me or should I
come back?

CHUCK AKERS

You look pretty gorgeous just the way you
are. You remind me of Ginny, that girl who
ran off with the drummer in the gospel band.

YODELER

Well, that'll never happen to me. Unless it's a
girl drummer.

She gets up and leaves. DONNA stands behind LEFTY and
combs his eyebrows and snips at them.

                         DONNA
        It's the end of an era when this show goes . . .
        won't be much of anything on radio but
        people yelling at you and computers playing
        music. It's a tragedy.

                      LEFTY (TO GUY)
        You know, I would think that a professional
        security man would be up at the stage door
        where he belongs, defending us against
        intruders, and not down here jawing about
        his allure to women.

                       GUY NOIR
        People with a clear conscience don't need
        much security. That's been my experience.
        And when I get the lowdown on this babe, I
        may or may not let you know about it. I may
        be out of here. We shall see.

25   INT. ONSTAGE—MOMENTS LATER

    GK at the announcer's podium, the JOHNSON GIRLS at stage
    center, MOLLY comes by and places scripts in their hands.
    ROBIN and LINDA stand behind GK, and the SHOE BAND.

                          GK
        And now the Johnson Girls remind you that
        this portion of our show is brought to you by
        the Ketchup Advisory Board. Ketchup—it's
        rich with natural mellowing agents.

    As he reads, MOLLY reaches over his shoulder, puts a script in
    place, yanks away the one he's reading.

                          GK
        And let's not forget those Powdermilk
        Biscuits either, right, Yolanda?

                          -63-

YOLANDA (READING)

When someone asks you where you're from and you tell them Minnesota, they think for a minute and then they say, "It gets cold there, doesn't it." And it does, of course.

RHONDA (READING)

Every year in Minnesota, nature makes a couple sincere attempts to kill you, and then we get the month of March, which God designed to show people who don't drink what a hangover is like.

YOLANDA

And that's why we Minnesotans are modest people. Because we've been through winter. If we ever got a gold medal, we would have it bronzed, so nobody would think that we think too highly of ourselves.

RHONDA

But we're stubborn. We believe in perseverance. Sticking to it. It's like becoming the Tallest Boy in the Fourth Grade. You stick around and eventually the prize will be yours.

GK

And when you need something to sustain you, reach for Powdermilk Biscuits, made from whole wheat that gives shy persons the strength to get up and do what needs to be done. Buy them in the big blue box with the picture of the biscuit on the cover or ready-made in the brown bag with the dark stains that indicate freshness.

ROBIN & LINDA & GK SING:
Has your family tried 'em,
Powdermilk?
O has your family tried 'em,
Powdermilk?
If your family's tried 'em
You know you've satisfied 'em,
They're the real hot item,
Powdermilk.

The BAND plays the Powdermilk Biscuit theme behind them,
as GK leans over YOLANDA.

GK
You want to do "Gold Watch & Chain," here?

YOLANDA
You have the words?

GK
You remember it.

RHONDA
Who's that woman over there? Another
girlfriend of yours?

YOLANDA (TO GK)
You sing lead and I'll come in.

GK
You sing lead. You always sing lead.

RHONDA
Another one of the girlfriends you ditched?

GK
Who?

RHONDA

Back there behind Dusty. Woman in a white
raincoat.

GK

Let's go.

The BAND ends the biscuit theme, to applause, as GK steps
up to the microphone.

GK

Lots of cards and letters from listeners this
week, and thank you for that. Always good
to know that people are listening and the
signal isn't just drifting around among the
pines and the blue jays.

RHONDA looks over GK's shoulder as he pretends to sort
through cards and letters on the podium.

GK

And here's a special request from young
Aaron Westendorp in Edina. He says, "I love
listening to your show and—"

RHONDA leans into the microphone.

RHONDA

He says, "I sure would love to hear those
Johnson Girls shake their hips and sing a
little,

(SHE SINGS)
Baby, baby, be my man . . . kiss me, touch me,
hold my hand . . .

GK
Just joking, he says.

RHONDA
Where does it say that?

GK
Right there. He'd like to hear Yolanda and me do
an old favorite here, called "Gold Watch & Chain."

(TO THE BAND)
Boys.

YOLANDA looks at GK with hesitation as the BAND strikes up
the tune. RHONDA, upstage, waves good-bye to the audience.
GK grabs a stool and sits. The band vamps for a few bars as GK
and YOLANDA look at each other. She is caught in uncertainty.
And then she gathers herself together and steps up and sings.

YOLANDA (SINGS)
Darling, how could I stay here without you
I have nothing to ease my poor heart
This old world would seem sad, love, without you
Tell me now that we never will part

YOLANDA & GK (SING)
Oh I'll pawn you my gold watch and chain, love
And I'll pawn you my gold wedding ring
I will pawn you this heart in my bosom
Only say that you'll love me again

CUT TO:

26   INT. FITZGERALD WINGS—SAME TIME

CHUCK AKERS stands in the wings, in a crowd, holding a
mandolin, and plays along softly.

YOLANDA (SINGS O.C.)
Oh, the white rose that grew in the garden
It died, dear, when you broke my heart

YOLANDA (SINGS O.C.) (CONT'D)
It bloomed on the day that I met you
But now we have fallen apart

The DANGEROUS WOMAN steps in beside CHUCK AKERS as he plays. He does not notice her, his escort to the next world. She waits patiently, as a mother waiting to drive a child to a birthday party.

YOLANDA & GK (SING O.C.)
Oh I'll pawn you my gold watch and chain, love
And I'll pawn you my gold wedding ring
I will pawn you this heart in my bosom
Only say that you'll love me again.

GUY NOIR slips in behind her and stands stock-still, eyeballing her, leaning slightly toward her and sniffing.

YOLANDA (SINGS O.C.)
Don't you know that I gave you my heart, dear,
It was given and can't be returned
You have left me to be with another
All my hopes and my bridges are burned.

CUT TO:

27   INT. STAGE—CONTINUOUS

YOLANDA and GK in duet.

YOLANDA & GK
Oh I'll pawn you my gold watch and chain, love
And I'll pawn you my gold wedding ring
I will pawn you this heart in my bosom
Only say that you'll love me again.
Only say that you'll love me again.
Only say that you'll love me again.

The song ends to applause, YOLANDA waves to the audience as STAGEHANDS bring in sound-effects table and gear, and MOLLY comes in with scripts.

GK

Thank you, Yolanda, and now let's come in
here with a message about duct tape.

He gestures questioningly to MOLLY (Duct tape?) and she vigorously nods yes, as she searches through the numerous stacks of paper she has carefully arranged in her left hand and right hand and under her left arm, as he wings it.

GK (O.C.)

Yes, duct tape. So many uses for it around the
house . . . loose windows, drafty windows . . .
things fall off, handles of things, levers,
grommets . . . you know how it is—

MOLLY is sorting through the array of scripts and papers in her hands, under her chin, between her knees. She is confident that the script is here, in her hands, and she searches quickly and with smooth dexterity.

GK (O.C.)

—things fall apart. It's the way of the world.
You put something in a safe place and two
minutes later you can't find it. Try taping it to
the wall with duct tape . . . it's like tying a
piece of string around your finger—

MOLLY, with batches of scripts and papers in her left hand, under her chin, in her mouth, reaches into her pocket for her glasses, puts them on, and in that moment, drops the papers under her left arm. They fly in all directions, and she tries to catch them, thus losing them all, creating a small blizzard of paper. Several musicians and a stagehand come to help her scoop up the debris. Meanwhile GK wings it.

GK

Duct tape . . . there's no end of uses for it. For
a quick fixer-upper, a strip of duct tape does
the job. So many things . . . leaking pipes—

The SOUND-EFFECTS (SFX) MAN does the sound of dripping.

GK

And the leak rots the wood so maybe your
whole kitchen counter comes loose.

SFX MAN does squeaking wood.

GK

Whole counter gets unattached from the wall.

SFX MAN, more wood squeaking. RHONDA steps in, inspired.

RHONDA

Maybe your orangutan was jumping up and
down on it.

SFX MAN does imitation of orangutan.

RHONDA

Maybe your Rottweiler got the orangutan all
riled up.

SFX MAN does imitation of Rottweiler.

GK

No, the Rottweiler was locked in the
basement.

SFX MAN closes SFX door, locks and bolts it.

GK
See? He's all locked up.

RHONDA
But the orangutan has a chain saw.

SFX MAN does orangutan starting up chainsaw.

RHONDA
And he cut a hole in the door and the
Rottweiler got out.

SFX MAN does orangutan, chainsaw, cutting wood,
Rottweiler.

RHONDA
And also the peacock.

SFX MAN does peacock, orangutan, Rottweiler.

RHONDA
And suddenly a helicopter came in overhead.

SFX MAN, helicopter.

RHONDA
Through the flock of Canadian geese. And
the helicopter startled the peacock.

SFX MAN, shriek of peacock.

YOLANDA
And he leaped at the orangutan.

SFX MAN, orangutan terror.

YOLANDA
And the orangutan threw the chainsaw.

SFX MAN, flying chainsaw.

RHONDA
Through the plate-glass window.

SFX MAN breaks glass in the sound box.

YOLANDA
And it hit the mailman, Harvey—

SFX MAN, scream.

YOLANDA
—who is bringing you a letter from your
ex-girlfriend. Which now you're never going
to read. So you won't know that she's still
angry at you for having dumped her—just
threw her away—the woman who loved
you—you met someone new and—how could
you do that? She'll never understand. And
duct tape isn't going to help you with that.

GK
No, I suppose not, but with two out of three
home chores—

YOLANDA now has GK in a tight spot. The audience realizes
that she is speaking directly to him and not kidding.

YOLANDA
Duct tape isn't going to make an honest man
out of you.

GK
No, it won't.

YOLANDA
And it isn't going to give you whatever it
was you were looking for. What *were* you
looking for?

GK
Looking for—

MOLLY has now found the script ("Aha!") and thrusts it at GK in triumph.

GK
—Got it!—duct tape. . . . Life is short and all repairs are temporary and it's almost just about the only thing that really works sometimes, duct tape.

MOLLY hands him one more script. He reads it from out of her hand.

GK
More of *A Prairie Home Companion* in a moment after we come in with a word about coffee. Yes, nothing keeps you focused quite like caffeine.

The BAND swings into a Latin rhythm, and JEARLYN dances onstage.

GK & JEARLYN (SINGING)
Smells so lovely when you pour it,
You will want to drink a quar't
Of coffee. It's delicious all alone, it's
Also good with doughnuts.
Black coffee.
Coffee stimulates your urges,
It is served in Lutheran churches,
Keeps the Swedes and Germans
Awake through the sermons.
Have a pot of it today,
I'm sure you'll say
It's awfully good coffee.

The jingle ends. MOLLY is at GK's elbow.

> GK
> And now while you get that cup of coffee,
> let's bring in Miss—

MOLLY takes his elbow, shakes her head, points to the wings
where CHUCK AKERS is emerging, whispers to GK.

> GK
> Let's bring in Mr. Chuck Akers right now
> with a number. Mr. Akers, how you doing
> tonight?

CHUCK AKERS, guitar on a strap around his neck, steps up to
a microphone, to audience applause.

> CHUCK AKERS
> Never better, thank you very much. No time
> like the present, that's what I say.

He touches up the tuning of the guitar as he talks.

> CHUCK AKERS
> I'd like to send this song out to all the fans
> who've meant so much to me through thirty
> years on this show. Doesn't seem like that long,
> but it has been. And, come Monday morning,
> Mrs. Akers and I are packing up the trailer and
> heading south, off on life's next adventure. So
> tonight's going to be good-bye for me.

There is strong applause.

CHUCK AKERS

Thank you very much. I never was much for
good-byes, but I would like to send this old
Carter Family song out to all the friends and
neighbors.

He strums.

CHUCK AKERS

My bark of life was tossing down
The troubled stream of time
When first I saw your smiling face
And youth was in its prime

Oh, I'll ne'er forget where e'er I roam
Where ever you may be
If ever I have had a friend
You have been that friend to me.

As he picks out a turnaround on the guitar, the BAND joins
him.

CHUCK AKERS

Misfortune nursed me as her child
And loved me fondly, too
I would have had a broken heart
Had it not been for you.

ROBIN & LINDA step up to a separate microphone to sing
with him on the chorus.

CHUCK AKERS & ROBIN & LINDA

Oh, I'll ne'er forget where e'er I roam
Where ever you may be
If ever I have had a friend
You have been that friend to me.

CHUCK AKERS
I now look back upon the past
Across life's troubled sea
And smile to think 'mid all life's scenes
You've been a friend to me.

CHUCK AKERS & ROBIN & LINDA & GK (BASS)
Oh, I'll ne'er forget where e'er I roam
Where ever you may be
If ever I have had a friend
You have been that friend to me.
If ever I have had a friend
You have been that friend to me.

The song ends to applause. CHUCK AKERS waves, bows, and
leaves the stage, and the camera follows him.

28   INT. FITZGERALD WINGS—SAME TIME

The LUNCH LADY stands in the wings, teary eyed, and
CHUCK AKERS walks past her and the STAGE MANAGER
into the crowd of musicians, where DUSTY and LEFTY are
waiting to go onstage, tended by MOLLY.

GK (O.C.)
Thank you, Chuck Akers. And right now,
let's come in with a word about ketchup.

(COMMERCIAL CONTINUES)

DUSTY (TO MOLLY)
Tell old Fish Face here that his butt is too big
for those pants of his and people can see his
crack and it isn't anything that a normal
person would ever care to see.

LEFTY looks back over his shoulder, trying to look at his butt.

LEFTY
Where?

DUSTY
In the back. That's where your crack is. Reach
back and you'll find it.

LEFTY
I don't see anything. Hey, Molly—

MOLLY
Don't ask.

LEFTY
Am I decent back there?

MOLLY
Don't ask me. I'm not your mother.

She walks away.

DUSTY
If you lost about fifty pounds, you might be.
Provided you didn't lose it from your head.

LEFTY eyes him and takes a step away.

LEFTY
Molly's expecting a baby.

DUSTY
So what?

LEFTY
Just stating a fact. Wonder who the daddy is?

DUSTY
Well, we all know it wasn't you.

LEFTY
She showed me her tattoo once.

DUSTY
Hell she did.

LEFTY
On her shoulder.

DUSTY
You're lying through your teeth.

LEFTY
Her left shoulder. Right here.

He points to a spot just below his collarbone.

DUSTY
Liar. That ain't her shoulder.

LEFTY
Whatever you want to call it.

DUSTY
You're ridiculous.

LEFTY
Ask her. Maybe she'll let you have a look at it.

DUSTY
What does it say?

LEFTY
It says Freedom.

DUSTY
Now I know you're lying.

Meryl Streep, Lily Tomlin, Garrison Keillor, and Maya Rudolph

Robert Altman on the set of *A Prairie Home Companion*

Meryl Streep and Lily Tomlin as The Johnson Girls
on stage at the Fitzgerald Theater

Garrison Keillor and Meryl Streep
on the stage of the Fitzgerald Theater

Lily Tomlin
as Rhonda
Johnson

Meryl Streep and
Lindsay Lohan
as Yolanda and
Lola Johnson

Lindsay Lohan
and Garrison
Keillor, backstage
at the Fitzgerald
Theater

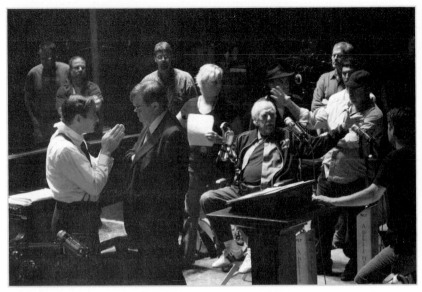

Kevin Kline and Garrison Keillor with Robert Altman (seated) and the crew of *A Prairie Home Companion* between takes on stage at the Fitzgerald Theater

Clockwise from upper left: Sue Scott, Kevin Kline, Garrison Keillor, Meryl Streep, and Lily Tomlin on the set at Mickey's Diner in St. Paul

Tim Russell (at the grill) and Kevin Kline
(at the counter), Mickey's Diner, St. Paul

Woody Harrelson and John C. Reilly
on the set at Mickey's Diner in St. Paul

John C. Reilly, Woody Harrelson, and Kevin Kline
on the set of *A Prairie Home Companion*

Woody Harrelson and John C. Reilly as Dusty and Lefty
on stage at the Fitzgerald Theater

Tommy Lee Jones and Virginia Madsen on the set
at the Fitzgerald Theater

Kevin Kline as Guy Noir

Kevin Kline as Guy Noir
on the stage of the Fitzgerald Theater

Virginia Madsen as The Dangerous Woman,
backstage at the Fitzgerald Theater

LEFTY
You just think whatever you want to think.

He sees LOLA approach and takes off his hat to her.

LEFTY
I hear you're going to sing us a song, Lola.
Looking forward to that.

LOLA
Hey, no problem.

LEFTY
Well, it sure means the world to your mom.
She always said you had talent.

LOLA
I don't know any of their songs. I only know
my songs.

LEFTY
So, sing one of them.

LOLA
They're mostly about death.

LEFTY (HE BRIGHTENS)
Well, a lot of good songs about death—

LOLA
Mine are about suicide.

LEFTY
Oh.

LOLA
Hanging yourself with an extension cord.
Carbon monoxide. That sort of thing.

DUSTY
I could do "Amazing Grace" with you.

LOLA
I know "Amazing Grace."

DUSTY
I could play guitar and we could get
everybody singing—

LEFTY
I'm not sure you knew this about my friend
Dusty here, but—

DUSTY
Oh shut up, would you?

LEFTY
He learned to sing gospel music at San
Quentin prison.

DUST
Just shut your pie hole—

LEFTY
That's where I found him. I was with Johnny
Cash, singing in prisons—

DUSTY
You're not funny, Lefty—

LEFTY
There were these heinous depraved
criminals, and—

DUSTY
She can tell you're lying. A child could tell—

LEFTY
But he sang "Amazing Grace." And it almost
made you forget what he'd done. Which I
don't want to talk about.

DUSTY
You're dumb enough to be twins.

LEFTY
I promised him on a Bible that I would never
tell and I won't. So let that be the end of it.

LOLA
When do you go on?

DUSTY
Soon as Fish Face stops talking.

LOLA
Thanks for the encouragement.

CUT TO:

29   INT. FITZGERALD THEATER—SAME TIME

GK
Back with more show right after this word
about shoes.

PAT DONOHUE & SHOE BAND (SING)
Talking shoes, talking Guy's,
Any two, any size.
From your ankle to your toes
At the bottom of your clothes
Talking shoes, talking Guy's.

GK at the microphone, motioning for DUSTY and LEFTY to
come out.

                              GK
        Guy's Shoes, they're made to last. And ask
        about the Guy's Cash Shoe, with the hole in
        the sole where you can stash your extra cash
        and keep it safe until you need it. Isn't that
        right, Lefty?

LEFTY stands at a microphone to GK's left. And DUSTY next
to him.

                             LEFTY
                   That's where I keep mine.

                              GK
        Good to have them with us here tonight.
        Please welcome the Old Trailhands
        themselves, the Puccinis of the Prairie, the
        Beethovens of the Bunkhouse—Dusty and
        Lefty!

APPLAUSE. DUSTY and LEFTY nod and bow, wave.

                             LEFTY
        Yes, sir, always good to be on the show,
        because, you know, it's mighty lonesome out
        there on the prairie. A cowboy gets tired of
        scenery after a while. You get sceneried out
        and you wish you had somebody to talk to.

                   (LOOKING AT DUSTY)
                   Somebody smart.

                              GK
               You miss people out there?

                    DUSTY
Yessir. Talking to a horse is not the same, and
my horse is pretty smart. He's good at math
and physics and chemistry, but I can't teach
him philosophy.

                    GK
You can't teach him philosophy?

                    DUSTY
Nope. You can't put Descartes before the
horse!

                    GK
Very good.

                    LEFTY
Speaking of horses, I want to thank all the
friends and neighbors who wrote in to say
how much they enjoyed "Come Ride My
Pony" that we sang last week. Thanks for all
your cards and letters. Meant a lot to me.

                                        CUT TO:

30   INT. BACKSTAGE—SAME TIME

                STAGE MANAGER
Somebody bring me a rifle, I'll kill the both of
them, the tall one first.

                    (ON P.A.)
Guy Noir to the stage.

Over his shoulder, the DANGEROUS WOMAN appears. She
stands at STAGE MANAGER's shoulder. He turns and walks
past her.

STAGE MANAGER
Hey Noir!

CUT TO:

31   INT. FITZGERALD WINGS—SAME TIME

People pass through the shot in the foreground and the
DANGEROUS WOMAN looks steadily at the camera as it
comes toward her.

DUSTY (O.C.)
One, two—you know what to do.

(SINGS)
I'm just an old cowboy with twigs in my hair
I'm two-thirds alligator and three-quarters bear
And one-half a liar but let it be known
I never told one lie that was not my own.

DUSTY & LEFTY (DUET)
Whoopitiyiyo git along little dogies.

CUT TO:

32   INT. FITZGERALD THEATER—SAME TIME

Onstage, LEFTY looks off at the DANGEROUS WOMAN who
is looking at him.

LEFTY (SINGS)
I eat when I'm hungry, I drink when I'm dry.
Don't boss me or cross me or I'll spit in your eye.
I think as I please and I say what I mean,
And I think all you women are the finest I've seen.

DUSTY & LEFTY (DUET)
Whoopitiyiyo git along little dogies.

DUSTY (SINGS)
I love the prairie, say what you will.
It's flat and it's dusty but I love it still
It's empty and lonely and tedious too
So maybe I'm crazy but what can I do.

DUSTY & LEFTY (DUET)
Whoopitiyiyo git along little dogies.

LEFTY
Here's the guitar solo coming up.

He picks out a short solo turnaround and looks into the wings.
The DANGEROUS WOMAN has disappeared.

LEFTY
Okay. Real good.

(HE SINGS)
I'm sure you can tell by the way we are dressed
We are two cowboys of the Wild West.
Cowboys whose shoes have stepped in manure
Heroes of song and of literature.
We ride in the snow and we ride in the rain
Just like Gene Autry, just like John Wayne
They were better cowboys than us and I mean it
But we are still living and that is convenient.

DUSTY & LEFTY (DUET)
Whoopitiyiyo git along little dogies.

33   INT. FITZGERALD WINGS—SAME TIME

LOLA sits on the security desk backstage, and GK sits in the
chair. She is holding a guitar and strumming it. Onstage, the
show continues, and we can hear the BAND playing.

LOLA

My mother said that you got into radio when
somebody was flying a kite? Somebody
whose clothes came off?

GK

It was a big kite towed behind a boat, and he
was on water skis.

LOLA

And he fell and he was dragged through the
water and his red swim trunks came off and
then the kite lifted him up in the air?

GK

A naked man, flying. It was quite a sight.

LOLA

Why didn't he pull up his shorts?

GK

He was hanging on to the kite.

LOLA

But how did that get you into radio?

GK

Well, that was how I met your dad. He was
flying the kite.

LOLA

My dad? He was the naked guy?

GK

Naked guy with his shorts around his ankles,
flying. It seemed like our chance to leave
town. So we headed for Chicago looking for
a job and we took turns driving. And he was

GK (CONT'D)
asleep in the backseat, when I pulled into a
truck stop in Oshkosh, Wisconsin—

LOLA
He told me about that.

GK
Yeah, I got out and went in to pay for the gas
and then he woke up and decided to go pee,
and then I came back and got in the car and
thought he was still asleep back there so I
pulled out on the highway and went to
Chicago and left him in Oshkosh. And he
went in the coffee shop and there was your
mother.

LOLA
So that's how I came to be born.

GK
It led up to it, yes.

LOLA
If you had looked in the backseat and seen he
wasn't there, I might not exist.

GK
Well, he and I weren't getting along all that
well, so I wasn't that anxious about him one
way or the other—

LOLA
That is so weird.

GK
Not if I look at you, then it's beautiful.

LOLA

Yeah, but to think that if you'd noticed he
was missing and turned around and gone
back to Oshkosh, I wouldn't exist.

GK

Makes it even more of a miracle that you do.

LOLA

So how'd you get into radio?

GK

I was doing a show called the *Baked Bean
Jamboree*—

LOLA

With my dad.

GK

Right.

LOLA

"Happy Baked Beans."

GK

You know it?

(SINGS WITH LOLA)

Happy Baked Beans are nutritious
Made the natural way.
Give you lots of fiber,
Try some, you will say:
They are nature's fruit, root-i-toot-toot-toot
Eat baked beans every day.

LOLA

But how did you get into radio?

                              GK
          Well . . . this was after the pontoon boat that
          capsized on the Mississippi—

                      STAGE MANAGER
          You are the worst person to tell a story I've
          ever heard in my life.

                              GK
                      It just takes time.

                      STAGE MANAGER
              Answer the question, would you.

                              GK
                  I'm getting around to it.

                             LOLA
          That's okay. You can tell me some other time.

          APPLAUSE (O.C.)

                      STAGE MANAGER
                      You're on. Go.

          GK jumps up.

                                              CUT TO:

34   INT. HALLWAY OUTSIDE DRESSING ROOM

      DONNA knocking at the door.

                            DONNA
              Chuck? I'm ready for you now. Chuck?

                                              CUT TO:

                             -89-

35   INT. DRESSING ROOM—SAME TIME

DONNA opens the door, freezes, has slow shocked reaction.

> DONNA
> Chuck? Are you decent? Chuck?

CUT TO:

36   INT. DRESSING ROOM—SAME TIME

CHUCK AKERS sits in a chair, head back, mouth open, eyes closed, his guitar in his lap, his arms draped awkwardly over it. He is wearing a shirt, undershorts, and socks, and there are candles burning on the table.

> DONNA
> Chuck?

She stands over him, studying him. She shakes his shoulder lightly. She touches his face.

> DONNA
> Oh my God.

She feels for his pulse. She puts her other hand on his chest, looking for a heartbeat.

> DONNA
> Oh Chuck. Why'd you have to go and do that
> now, ya old bugger? This was supposed to be
> your last show. You were supposed to get a
> trophy. . . . Now what am I supposed to do?
> Huh? Just tell me that.

DONNA pulls a sheet over CHUCK AKERS.

CUT TO:

DONNA closes the dressing room door and puts up a sign:
Do Not Disturb. She bows her head for a moment, takes a
deep breath, then walks away.

CUT TO:

The DANGEROUS WOMAN stands at the security desk, wearing
her Twins baseball cap and dark glasses. GUY NOIR sits behind
the desk, rummaging in the top drawer for a pencil and paper.

> DANGEROUS WOMAN
> It's time for me to go.

> GUY NOIR (NOT LOOKING UP)
> Okay.

> DANGEROUS WOMAN
> Look at me.

> GUY NOIR (NOT LOOKING UP)
> What's going on?

> DANGEROUS WOMAN
> Look at me.

He looks up. She leans forward.

> DANGEROUS WOMAN
> Listen very carefully and don't be afraid. I
> am the angel Asphodel. I come to do my
> work and bring mercy into the world and to
> carry out the Lord's will and honor His holy
> name. With every breath of my being may I
> proclaim the glory of the Lord.

The DANGEROUS WOMAN takes off her dark glasses and
baseball cap and shakes out her hair.

> GUY NOIR (DAZED)
> If you want to be an angel, sweetheart, hey—
> I'm all for it. You're angelic enough for me. I
> say, spread your wings and fly.

> DANGEROUS WOMAN
> This is a revelation—

> GUY NOIR
> Hey, for you and me both! Mind if I ask a
> question?

> DANGEROUS WOMAN
> I know your question and the answer is no.

> GUY NOIR
> You're not, huh?

> DANGEROUS WOMAN
> No.

CUT TO:

39   INT. DRESSING ROOM—MOMENTS LATER

In dim light, GK sits in the corner, his jacket off, his feet up on
a chair.

> DANGEROUS WOMAN (O.C.)
> I used to listen to your show. Until the night I
> died. My name was Lois Peterson.

The DANGEROUS WOMAN sits on the dressing table, her
legs dangling down.

DANGEROUS WOMAN

I was driving to this cabin up north and you
were telling a story and I started laughing
and I lost control of the car and it skidded
into the ditch and flipped over and, as it did,
the thought crossed my mind that the story
wasn't that funny. And then I was standing
in this tall grass and looking down at my
own body. My head at a weird angle. My
neck broken when the car flipped. I was on
my way to the cabin to meet my lover Larry.
We had planned this for two months and
your story caused me to lose control and I
died. My head was flopped over like a
chicken's. You sort of killed me, in a way.
Isn't that interesting?

GK

I'm so sorry.

DANGEROUS WOMAN

Of course you are. But I don't miss my life. I
did for a while but then I got over it. I sort of
miss licorice. And martinis. All those
different cheeses they have. I remember these
soft white cheeses that Larry and I would
melt and we'd sit out on the porch and dip
slices of bread in it.

GK

Fondue.

DANGEROUS WOMAN

I've been trying to think of that word. What
is it?

GK

Fondue.

DANGEROUS WOMAN
It was famous. Is that the word? It was good.
Tasted good.

GK
The melted cheese?

DANGEROUS WOMAN
Yes.

GK
Maybe you mean fabulous.

DANGEROUS WOMAN
Fabulous. Yes. Fabulous. Fabulous. I like the
B there. Fabulous. But I'm okay with being an
angel. No regrets. Not really.

GK
You're really an angel?

DANGEROUS WOMAN
Of course.

GK
What do you do? Well, that's a dumb
question . . .

DANGEROUS WOMAN
I comfort people who are desperately sad.
And I take people up to God. That's why I
came. But you know, I always wondered
about that story and why it was funny.

GK
What story was it?

DANGEROUS WOMAN
It was about penguins.

GK
Oh. Right. The two penguins standing on the
ice floe.

DANGEROUS WOMAN
Yes.

GK
And one says, "You look like you're wearing
a tuxedo." And the other penguin says, "Who
says I'm not?"

DANGEROUS WOMAN
Is there more?

GK
No.

DANGEROUS WOMAN
That's the joke?

GK
Yes.

DANGEROUS WOMAN
Why is that funny?

GK
It's funny because people laugh at it.

DANGEROUS WOMAN
I'm not laughing.

GK
You're an angel.

DANGEROUS WOMAN
My husband loved your show. He was so
torn up after I died, he couldn't bear to listen
to your show ever again.

GK
You were on your way to see him?

DANGEROUS WOMAN
No, I was going to see Larry.

GK
Oh.

DANGEROUS WOMAN
My lover.

She stands up and walks to the door and turns.

DANGEROUS WOMAN
Married woman, shacking up with another
guy, and here I am. Go figure. God has his
own way of looking at things, that's for sure.
I used to like to sing. I don't even remember
how it's done. You open your mouth, right?
I've seen that . . .

She opens and closes her mouth. She smiles at him. She opens
her mouth and forms an O shape. And then a crying shape.
She tries out different shapes: small and pursed, wide, twisted,
various grimaces.

GK
Can I go upstairs now?

DANGEROUS WOMAN
Oh, of course. I didn't come to get you.

GK

They're probably wondering where I went.

DANGEROUS WOMAN

You're okay. What did the second penguin
say?

GK

"Who says I'm not?"

DANGEROUS WOMAN

Okay.

He gets up to go.

GK

See you later.

DANGEROUS WOMAN

Take your time.

CUT TO:

39A INT. FITZGERALD THEATER—SAME TIME

GK strides to the microphone.

GK

Thank you, Guys' All Star Shoe Band, and
that brings us up to the hour, time to break
for station identification. Don't go away—
we'll be back with more right after this.

The curtain descends as we hear the WLT studio announcer on
the P.A.

STUDIO ANNOUNCER
This is WLT, the Friendly Neighbor station,
with studios in St. Paul and Minneapolis.

A recorded commercial follows, faded down, as MOLLY and
STAGE MANAGER come out to the podium onstage, followed
by GUY NOIR. MOLLY sorts through the welter of papers on
the podium, pulls out most of them, takes some new pages
from the STAGE MANAGER, inserts those in the stack.

MOLLY
You didn't see any of the Soderbergs in the
audience—

GK
Nope.

GK is going through papers, reordering them.

STAGE MANAGER
If you do, have them stand up. Talk about
what great bosses they are and how loyal
they are to the show and how much we all
love 'em. Get the audience to give 'em a
big round of applause. Humiliate 'em.

MOLLY
Al—

STAGE MANAGER
Better yet, bring 'em up here and we'll give
'em that trophy.

MOLLY
Hard to believe that next week we've got to
start looking for work—

GUY NOIR
I've got plenty of work.

MOLLY
What?

GUY NOIR
Lot of things. You name it.

STAGE MANAGER
You got Lola down for a song?

GK
I didn't see her name.

STAGE MANAGER
Well, I promised her mother.

GK
Okay. Just tell me when.

STAGE MANAGER returns to his desk.

GUY NOIR
Could I have a word with you?

He sidles up next to the podium, looks around.

GUY NOIR
We've got a situation here that we're
monitoring and I thought you ought to be
apprised of it.

GK
You mean, the woman in the white coat?

GUY NOIR
You saw her?

GK
Uh-huh.

GUY NOIR
You spoke to her?

GK
No.

GUY NOIR
If you see her in the audience, give me the
high sign.

He demonstrates, hand behind back, waggling fingers.

GUY NOIR
See how that works? Give me the sign and
use a code word. Like *indemnity*. Better yet,
Granite Falls.

GK
How does that work?

GUY NOIR
"We'd like to do a song for a listener from
Granite Falls."

He demonstrates hand behind back and finger waggle.

GK
Code, huh. That's how I got into radio, you
know that?

GUY NOIR
I'm not kidding.

GK

I was a deckhand on an ore boat, the *Joseph J. O'Connell,* on Lake Superior. Did I ever tell you that story?

GUY NOIR
Many times.

GK

It was November. We were taking forty-foot waves across the bow and they were hitting the wheelhouse and the navigation equipment was out and I was on the bridge and the old man says to me, "Get on the radio and stay on the radio so the Coast Guard can give us a location."

GUY NOIR
So you went on the radio and you sang and told jokes for two hours and the ship made it safely to port.

GK
Right. Two hours. So I told you that.

GUY NOIR
Granite Falls.

He demonstrates finger waggle again and exits.

MOLLY
Thirty seconds. What are you going to do for work?

GK
Me?

MOLLY
Yeah. You.

GK
I want a job where I don't have to talk at all.

MOLLY
Why?

GK
That's why.

MOLLY
What do you mean?

GK
Exactly.

MOLLY is watching the STAGE MANAGER in the wings and
gives GK the sign.

MOLLY
You're on.

GK
Welcome back to *A Prairie Home Companion*
brought to you by New Munich beer.
Remember when parties used to be fun—
back when everyone drank beer? Before
people got so serious about wine? Try New
Munich. It's cheap and—darn it—it makes
people happy.

GK (SINGS WITH BAND)
Have a glass and tell a joke a-
Bout a man who danced the polka
And remember that the party has to end, my friend.
Adieu, adieu, kind friends, adieu.

GK (SINGS WITH BAND) (CONT'D)
But first let's have another brew.
I can't wait to take you home, my dear.
Boy O boy, New Munich beer.

The song ends.

GK
Coming up next, the Johnson Girls and the
Old Trailhands, Dusty and Lefty, and right
now, Miss Jearlyn Steele . . .

40   INT. FITZGERALD THEATER—SAME TIME

Onstage, JEARLYN stands listening to the SHOE BAND, a
slow blues, and then she picks up her cue and sings.

JEARLYN
The day is short
The night is long
Why do you work so hard
To get what you don't even want?
We work so hard to get ahead in the game
Give up half our lives until we've won.
And one night we sit on the edge of the bed
And we think, "Lord, what have I done?"

The day is short
The night is long
Why do you work so hard
To get what you don't even want.

She turns to the BAND, and the PIANIST plays a break.

DISSOLVE TO:

41   INT. FITZGERALD WINGS—SAME TIME

The STAGE MANAGER is looking up at the clock, his lips move as he calculates minutes remaining in the broadcast.

> STAGE MANAGER
> How can that be? We're running slow?
> Where'd we lose six minutes?

The DANGEROUS WOMAN enters and stands behind him, looking out to the stage.

> JEARLYN (SINGS O.C.)
> The man in the suit kisses his babies good-bye.
> "Daddy's going on a trip, honey, don't you cry."
> And he's gone for a week then he's home for a day.
> Pretty soon they don't cry when Daddy goes away.
>
> The day is short
> The night is long
> Why do you work so hard
> To get what you don't even want.

CUT TO:

42   INT. FITZGERALD THEATER—SAME TIME

JEARLYN stands all the way downstage, illuminated in a single spot.

> JEARLYN (SINGS)
> Go to the mall and go from store to store.
> Everybody's killing time until death walks through the door
> Then you look around at all your merchandise
> And you see you've paid much too high a price.

> JEARLYN (SINGS) (CONT'D)
> The day is short
> The night is long
> Why do you work so hard
> To get what you don't even want.

CUT TO:

43   INT. HALLWAY OUTSIDE DRESSING ROOM—MOMENTS LATER

The door with the Do Not Disturb sign slowly opens and DUSTY emerges, pale and shaken. Pulls cigarette out of pack in pocket. Lights it. Takes a deep drag. Looks off to right.

> GUY NOIR (O.C.)
> *Hey!*

DUSTY jumps, drops cigarette, bends down to get it, comes up red-faced.

> GUY NOIR
> No smoking, mister.

> DUSTY
> Chuck Akers is dead. He's gone.

> GUY NOIR
> I don't follow your reasoning there.

> DUSTY
> I said Chuck's dead.

> GUY NOIR
> Who's dead?

> DUSTY
> Chuck.

GUY NOIR
When?

DUSTY
Now.

GUY NOIR
He just died now?

DUSTY
I don't know when he died. How would I
know that? I wasn't there.

GUY NOIR
What was the approximate time of death?

DUSTY
See for yourself. He's in there.

GUY NOIR
In the green room? (HE GLANCES
AROUND) Who else knows about this?

DUSTY
I have no idea.

GUY NOIR
Cause if other people know and they're not
saying anything, I'd like to know about that.
Excuse me.

GUY NOIR eases the door open and steps in, then steps out.

GUY NOIR
Jeez. He was walking around exchanging
gases with the atmosphere half an hour ago.

> DUSTY
> Call the cops.

> GUY NOIR
> When it's time, I will. Just . . . don't mention
> this to anybody, okay? I'm gonna secure the
> area. You got another cigarette?

DUSTY pulls out another cigarette.

> GUY NOIR
> Thanks. 'Preciate it.

He looks left and right as he clicks his lighter. Holds up the
flame. Notices cigarette in his mouth is filter end out. Switches
it around. Lights. Smokes.

CUT TO:

44   INT. FITZGERALD THEATER—SAME TIME

GK onstage, as musicians change behind him. ROBIN and
LINDA WILLIAMS come into position, wearing cowboy
outfits, with guitars.

> GK
> Let's see who we have here in our audience
> today . . . the Barthelmes are here from
> Minneapolis, and the Wyle family, Sue and
> Bucky. And they've requested "Yonny
> Yonson's Wedding" so let's bring up Robin
> and Linda to help me out and we'll send this
> out to all the Norwegian bachelor farmers
> out there.

The BAND launches into the intro.

GK (SINGS)

Oh we had a lovely party at the Norway lodge last night
Every last Norwegian was there with an appetite
Their hair was brushed, their teeth was combed, they smelled of
    fungicide
At Johnny and Christina Johnson's wedding.

We had a quart of whiskey and a couple kegs of beer.
And everyone drank faster as we watched it disappear.
Then Svendson got out the aquavit and everybody cheered
At Johnny and Christina Johnson's wedding.

GK (SINGS WITH ROBIN & LINDA)

There was Clarence Nilsson and Hjalmar Nilsson and Gladys
Nilsson and Lois Nilsson
And Ray Nilsson and Evelyn Nilsson and Nils Nilsson he was there
too.

CUT TO:

45   INT. JOHNSON GIRLS' DRESSING ROOM—SAME TIME

LOLA and RHONDA stand in front of the mirror. YOLANDA
sits at the makeup table, looking in the mirror.

RHONDA
Just do what I do, baby.

She sings and swings into a simple Supremes step routine.

RHONDA (SINGS)
Oh baby . . . yes yes
Baby baby . . . do it like this.

LOLA
What's this?

RHONDA
Don't talk. Dance.

(SINGS)
Baby baby please come in
I've been waiting to begin
Kiss me sweet and kiss me slow
And don't stop til I say so.

Baby baby . . . yes yes
Oh baby . . . just like this
Baby baby . . . you know how
Oh baby . . . don't stop now.

They turn slowly, keeping time, snapping their fingers, singing
*oooo*s in R&B backbeat.

RHONDA
Your mama wrote this song.

LOLA (TO YOLANDA)
You didn't.

YOLANDA smiles.

LOLA
Wow.

RHONDA
We recorded this and it was just about to
come out and the Doo-Dads stole it from us.
Put it out and it went to number one and we
got a lawyer and he took us for everything
we had.

LOLA
Oh my God.

                    RHONDA (SINGS)
            Oooo baby . . . you're my man
            You do what no other can
            I'm a girl who's hard to please
            You bring me to my knees
            (Oooooo)

They strike a pose and then fall apart, laughing.

                        LOLA
                Hey, we've got an act.

                       RHONDA
            For nightclubs. Vegas. No sense wasting it on
            radio.

YOLANDA is smiling.

                        LOLA
            Let's sing it on the show, Mama. The
            Johnsons!

                      YOLANDA
            I just love looking at you, you know that?
            Such a miracle.

She looks lovingly at LOLA.

                      YOLANDA
            All the bad-luck stuff doesn't matter. Because
            I got you. A daughter.

They embrace.

RHONDA (SINGS)
Oh baby . . . sing my song
We been waiting much too long
Lock the door, turn out the light
O yes . . . tonight's the night.

45A INT. FITZGERALD STAGE—SAME TIME

GK
Prince of Pizza, the frozen pizza that tastes
homemade. With real Minnesota mozzarella
and sausage.

(HE SINGS, TO TUNE OF "LA DONNA E MOBILE")
One Prince of Pizza slice
Puts me in paradise,
Sausage and extra cheese
Onions and anchovies,
You can stay home
And feel you're in Rome
No need to go ta
Italy, you can eat prettily here in Minnesota.

Prince of Pizza.

46   INT. HALLWAY OUTSIDE DRESSING ROOM—MOMENTS
LATER

LUNCH LADY is knocking on the door with the Do Not
Disturb sign.

LUNCH LADY
Chuck? Honey? It's me, Evie. Ready or not,
here I come.

She opens the door quietly.

LUNCH LADY
I'm looking for a big hot dog to put in my
bun, you old dog you.

She slips in and closes the door.

LUNCH LADY (O.C.)
Wake up, sugar.

She screams.

CUT TO:

47   INT. CHUCK'S DRESSING ROOM

DANGEROUS WOMAN embraces the LUNCH LADY.

DANGEROUS WOMAN
It's okay. It's okay. It's okay. It's all okay.

LUNCH LADY
How can he be dead?

DANGEROUS WOMAN
He just went away, that's all.

LUNCH LADY
My Chuck . . . my baby . . .

DANGEROUS WOMAN
The death of an old man is not a tragedy.

LUNCH LADY (WEEPING)
I—don't—want him to—go.

DANGEROUS WOMAN
Forgive him for his shortcomings, and thank
him for his love and care . . .

The LUNCH LADY is blubbering, speechless, in the arms of the DANGEROUS WOMAN.

                    DANGEROUS WOMAN
          Tell him he will be remembered, and turn
          away and live your life.

                    LUNCH LADY (CRYING)
                Good-bye, baby.

                (TO DANGEROUS WOMAN)
          You got anything to drink? Like a rum and coke?

48   INT. HALLWAY OUTSIDE DRESSING ROOM—MOMENTS
LATER

GK stands at the JOHNSON GIRLS' dressing room door, listening to them sing inside with LOLA.

                    YOLANDA & RHONDA & LOLA (O.C.)
                Oooo baby . . . you're my man
                You do what no other can
                I'm a girl who's hard to please
                You bring me to my knees.
                Oh baby . . . sing my song
                We been waiting much too long
                Lock the door, turn out the light
                Oh yes . . . tonight's the night.

He knocks lightly on the door.

                                        CUT TO:

49   INT. HALLWAY OUTSIDE DRESSING ROOM—MOMENTS
LATER

YOLANDA stands in the doorway. Camera looks over GK's shoulder as he speaks.

YOLANDA
You heard about the Soderbergs selling the
radio station.

GK
Yeah, I heard—

YOLANDA
Are you okay?

GK
Of course.

YOLANDA
Kind of a bizarre feeling, isn't it?

GK
What?

YOLANDA
The silence.

GK
What are we supposed to say?

YOLANDA
Are you going to say something?

GK
On the air?

YOLANDA
Of course. "Thanks for listening" . . .
something. "Good-bye"?

GK
I hate good-byes. I don't believe in them.

YOLANDA

What do you do when you leave someone's
house?? Just turn around and walk away?

GK

I just don't want to make a big weepy speech
about—

YOLANDA

That's it!!! You're afraid you would cry!!!

GK

I wouldn't either.

YOLANDA

That's right. You wouldn't. You know, maybe
that's why you and I broke up when we did.
Because I knew that if I waited, you wouldn't
cry anyway. Does that make sense?

GK

No.

50   INT. FITZGERALD STAGE—SAME TIME

Musicians coming on- and offstage, YOLANDA and
RHONDA come onstage as GK speaks at the podium, and
ROBIN and LINDA stand at the microphone.

GK

Tonight's show brought to you by
Bebopareebop Rhubarb Pie and
Bebopareebop Rhubarb Pie Filling. Wouldn't
this be a good time for a piece of rhubarb pie?

BAND strikes up "Shortnin' Bread."

GK & ROBIN & LINDA (SING)
One little thing can revive a guy
And that is a piece of rhubarb pie.
Serve it up, nice and hot,
Maybe things aren't as bad as you thought.
Oh, Mama's little baby loves rhubarb, rhubarb
Mama's little baby loves rhubarb pie.
Mama's little baby loves rhubarb, rhubarb,
Mama's little baby loves rhubarb pie.

GK
And now here's Yolanda and Rhonda, our
very own Johnson Girls!

The audience applauds.

YOLANDA
Thank you so much. This is a song we wrote
for our mama who brought us up, with no
luxuries, no vacation trips, no vacations,
period. Just one luxury and that was music.
No matter how tired she was, she loved to
hear us kids sing and—

She is momentarily choked up.

YOLANDA puts a hand on RHONDA's shoulder.

YOLANDA
She did the laundry in one of those old
washing machines with a wringer. She fished
out the wet sheets and towels with a big
stick and hung it all on the line. She did
everything for us, made our clothes, put up
preserves, a hundred jars of corn and beets
and tomatoes. This is for you, Mama.

YOLANDA & RHONDA (SINGING)
Good-bye to my mama, my uncles and aunts,
One after another, they went to lie down
In the green pastures beside the still waters
And make no sound.
Their arms that held me for so many years
Their beautiful voices no longer I'll hear
They're in Jesus' arms and he's talking to them
In the rapturous new Jerusalem
And I know they're at peace in a land of delight
But I miss my Mama tonight.

DISSOLVE TO:

51   INT. BACKSTAGE—SAME TIME

GK, LEFTY, and DUSTY stand in the wings, watching.

YOLANDA & RHONDA
Good-bye, Eleanor, and Aunt Franny and Jo
Good-bye, Uncle Jim, and Elsie and Don,
Good-bye to my mama who went to lie down
And now is gone.

Whose hands are these so rough and hard
Nails all torn from toil and care?
Who cleaned the house and kept the yard?
Touched my cheek and stroked my hair?

Thank you, Mama, the Lord give you peace.
Bless your voice and the songs you've sung.
Blessed your arms and your hands and your knees.
How you loved us when we were young.

CUT TO:

52   INT. BACKSTAGE—SAME TIME

The DANGEROUS WOMAN walks past, stops, watches for a
moment. Continues.

> YOLANDA & RHONDA (SING)
> The Lord's my shepherd, I'll not want.
> I have my mama, my uncles and aunts.
> Waters so still and the pastures so green.
> Goodness and mercy following me.
> Goodness and mercy following me.

The BAND is playing onstage and musicians are standing in
the shadows offstage, the reflection of stage light on their
faces. LEFTY and DUSTY are waiting. JEARLYN is by his side.

> DISSOLVE TO:

53   INT. FITZGERALD WINGS—SAME TIME

The STAGE MANAGER is looking up at the clock. His lips
move as he calculates minutes remaining in the broadcast.

> STAGE MANAGER
> Get Chuck up here.

> DUSTY
> Don't forget our song.

> STAGE MANAGER
> What's this one about? Horse hockey?

> DUSTY
> Not about horses at all.

On the STAGE MANAGER's desk the phone light flashes red
and he picks it up.

> STAGE MANAGER
> Yeah? . . . He's here? . . . Okay. . . . Thanks.

He hangs up the phone.

> STAGE MANAGER
> The axeman is here.

He turns.

> STAGE MANAGER
> Hey what happened to that trophy we were
> gonna give to Chuck? Who took it?

CUT TO:

54   EXT. FITZGERALD THEATER—FRONT OF BUILDING

Nighttime. The lobby and glassed entry are brightly lit. The
marquee advertises *A Prairie Home Companion*. A black car is
parked at the curb. The chauffeur stands by the open rear
door.

The AXEMAN is walking from the car to the entry and
entering the front door. He is slender, tanned, fashionable,
handsome, in a black suit, black shirt, dressed like a magazine
model. The TICKET LADY asks him a question but he smiles
and walks in. She follows him for a few steps. A young male
USHER steps toward him and half blocks his way.

55   INT. FITZGERALD LOBBY—SAME TIME

The AXEMAN looks around. A few fans around the souvenir
stand turn to look at him, assuming that he is a famous person
but unable to put a name to him.

> USHER
> Do you have a ticket?

                              AXEMAN
                    I'm with the company.

He gives the usher a smile and walks past him.

                                                    CUT TO:

56   INT. FITZGERALD LOBBY—SAME TIME

The AXEMAN strolls through the archway to the inner
hallway. He looks to his left.

                         GUY NOIR (O.C.)
                         Mr. Cruett?

The AXEMAN studies him for a moment.

                              AXEMAN
                    I don't believe we've met.

GUY NOIR stands, hand in pocket, facing him. He pulls out a
cigar.

                            GUY NOIR
                 Guy Noir, vice president for security and
                 data acquisition.

                              AXEMAN
                    Show almost over?

GUY NOIR lights the cigar and puffs, and takes a deep drag
and blows smoke.

                            GUY NOIR
                            Almost.

AXEMAN
Well, just in time then. Show's been going
how long? Somebody said fifty years.

GUY NOIR
Almost. Thirty-something.

AXEMAN
Weird. Like a time warp.

GUY NOIR
We've got the luxury box waiting for you.
Right this way—

AXEMAN
Who's the guy up there?

GUY NOIR turns and looks.

The bust of F. Scott Fitzgerald sits on a ledge above their
heads.

GUY NOIR (O.C.)
He's a guy who used to come to shows here.
F. Scott Fitzgerald. Novelist. Grew up in St.
Paul.

AXEMAN (O.C.)
What kind of novels?

GUY NOIR (O.C.)
Romantic ones. *The Great Gatsby.*

AXEMAN (O.C.)
Oh. I don't read romance. No time. Where
am I going?

GUY NOIR (O.C.)
Right in here.

CUT TO:

57   INT. FITZGERALD LOBBY—SAME TIME

GUY NOIR opens a door and the AXEMAN enters a room
with a large glass window looking directly at the stage. It's a
dim room with a couch and several easy chairs and a table
with glasses and liquor decanters on it. GUY NOIR reaches up
and turns down the volume on the wall monitor.

GUY NOIR
Usually we've got five or six clients in here,
sponsors and so on, but—

AXEMAN
Nice plasterwork around the proscenium.
We'll have to remember to save a piece of
that. I wish we'd taped this show. Videotape.
For historical purposes. Send it to a museum.

GUY NOIR
Let me fix you a drink.

AXEMAN
Just water. No ice.

GUY NOIR pours a glass of water from a pitcher and hands it
to the AXEMAN.

GUY NOIR
So what can I tell you about the show?

AXEMAN
I know all I need to know about the show.

GUY NOIR
You sure about that?

AXEMAN
I am. Theater's got to come down. We've got
a Prince of Pizza drive-in coming in here in
three months.

GUY NOIR
Not going to change your mind?

AXEMAN
Man's got to do what has to be done, Mr.
Noir.

GUY NOIR
Lot of good people up there, on the stage . . .
lot of them. I mean, I'm a man of the world
like yourself, but . . . these folks put their
lives into this.

AXEMAN
Now they can put their lives into something
else. Always something to put your life into,
right? No, it's like Scripture says, you've got
to lose your life before you can find it.

GUY NOIR
Scripture is guiding you here?

AXEMAN
The company is owned by people of faith,
Mr. Noir.

The AXEMAN sits down on an easy chair.

AXEMAN
Before I came to the Lord, I played in a band
myself. The Dukes of Rhythm. We put our
lives into it and we were awful. Bunch of
drunks thinking we knew it all. And then,
thank God, we were rescued by the simple
fact of getting fired. It was a blessing. Lost
my guitar to a repo man. You lose one life,
you find another. Praise the Lord.

GUY NOIR
I'll be right back.

He wheels around and exits past the camera.

CUT TO:

58   INT. FITZGERALD LOBBY—SAME TIME

GUY NOIR closes the door quietly behind him. He walks
down the hall past two ushers sitting in chairs, reading books,
and stops at the concession stand, hearing . . . something . . .
and looks over the counter. MOLLY sits on the floor within the
little cubicle, listening to the radio.

GUY NOIR
Hi there.

MOLLY
Hi. I never listened to it on the radio before.

GUY NOIR
Oh?

MOLLY
Who's the guy in the booth?

GUY NOIR
He's the hangman. The iceman.

MOLLY
Funny. People sitting at home and listening . . .
and they don't know: it's the last one. You
know? It's like, you always think there's going
to be more after this. But maybe not.

GUY NOIR
Everything has an ending, sweetheart.

MOLLY
My aunt Evelyn listened to it every Saturday.
Five o'clock, she was right there by the radio.
Until they put her in the home. In the home,
supper was at five. So she took the radio to
the dining room. It wasn't plugged in but by
then she wasn't either, so . . . she was happy
just looking at the dial and moving the knobs.

GUY NOIR
I listened to it back in my gumshoe days.
Saturday night, I'd be tailing some two-timing
husband who was floozing around with his
paramour down at the Romeo Motel, I'd sit in
the parking lot listening to the symphony of
the bedsprings, and I'd tune in *A Prairie Home
Companion* to take my mind off it.

GUY NOIR grimaces and turns away.

GUY NOIR
Hey, I need your help.

GUY NOIR pulls a sheet of paper from his inside jacket pocket
and puts it against the wall and writes on it.

CLOSEUP of note, as he writes: "ANGEL—MAN IN THE BOOTH. MAKE HIM GO AWAY."

GUY NOIR
Take this to that beautiful woman in the white raincoat. Backstage.

MOLLY
The one with the Mount Rushmore T-shirt?

GUY NOIR
You got it.

MOLLY
Anything else?

GUY NOIR
You know how to jigger the master clock?

MOLLY
Al would kill me.

GUY NOIR
I just need a few minutes.

MOLLY
The clock is sacred. It's like the law and the prophets.

GUY NOIR
I just need you to add about five minutes.

MOLLY
Guy—

GUY NOIR
Five minutes.

59   INT. ONSTAGE—MOMENTS LATER

DUSTY, LEFTY, and GK at the microphones. Musicians
scurrying into place behind them. The DUCT TAPE fly lowers
as the GUY'S SHOES fly rises.

                         GK
        It's Saturday night on *A Prairie Home
        Companion*—lots more to come—and right
        now, they've just come in off the range with a
        brand-new song, it's the old Trailhands,
        Dusty and Lefty!

Audience applause, as the musicians kick in.

                        DUSTY
        Here's a brand-new number. Want to send
        this out to our good friends listening out
        around Maple Plain and Renville and the
        folks in Glenwood, and all of your good
        people out there.

                   LEFTY (SINGS)
The blind man's seeing-eye dog pissed on the blind man's shoe,
The blind man said, "Here, Rover, here's a piece of beef for you."
His wife said, "Don't reward him, you can't just let that pass."
The blind man said, "I've got to find his mouth so I can kick him in
the ass."

The BAND plays a chorus.

                                            CUT TO:

60   INT. BACKSTAGE—SAME TIME

The STAGE MANAGER stands at his desk and stares at
DUSTY and LEFTY onstage.

STAGE MANAGER

Doesn't make much difference at this point.
Piss, ass—what the hell? Damn show is on
the way out anyway.

DUSTY (SINGS)

When God created woman
He gave her not two breasts but three
But the middle one got in the way
So God performed surgery.
Woman stood before God
With the middle breast in her hand
She said, "What can we do with the useless boob?"
And God created man.

The BAND plays a chorus.

STAGE MANAGER

Boobs—why not? Tits, ass—more the merrier.
Bring it on.

RHONDA

What about boobs?

RHONDA has strolled in to watch the end of the show.

STAGE MANAGER

They're singing a song about boobs and poop
and who knows what? Hey. Why not?

He picks up the papers on his desk and tosses them up high in
the air.

STAGE MANAGER

Let's have a drink. Let's get shit-faced.

RHONDA

You do it and I'll watch.

61   INT. ONSTAGE—CONTINUOUS

DUSTY and LEFTY are hamming it up like a couple of song-and-dance men, and the audience is whooping and laughing.

> LEFTY (SINGS)
> I turned sixty the other day
> And everybody was there
> I was all dressed up in a brand-new suit
> Sitting in my big armchair
> When a beautiful young naked woman
> Stood up in front of the group.
> She offered me some super sex
> And I said, "I'll take the soup."

Big cymbal crash and whoops and the BAND plays a chorus.

CUT TO:

62   INT. BACKSTAGE—SAME TIME

STAGE MANAGER and RHONDA in the wings.

> STAGE MANAGER
> Guess we can all shake our tits now, huh?

STAGE MANAGER puts his arms around RHONDA.

> STAGE MANAGER
> It's over, kid. They're pulling the plug. The
> show's gone.

> YOLANDA (O.C.)
> Al . . . Chuck's dead. He died in his dressing
> room.

STAGE MANAGER stands stock-still, in disbelief.

> RHONDA
> He went down to his dressing room to take a
> nap and he just never woke up. Sorry, Al.

STAGE MANAGER takes a deep breath and turns back to his
post.

> STAGE MANAGER
> I was supposed to go down and get him and
> I forgot all about him.

CUT TO:

63   INT. ONSTAGE—MOMENTS LATER

> DUSTY (SINGS)
> Ole went to the neighborhood dance
> And he won the big door prize
> It was a toilet brush and he took it home
> And the next week one of the guys
> Said, "Ole, how's that toilet brush?
> Ole said, "Thank you, neighbor.
> The toilet brush, it works pretty good.
> But I prefer toilet paper."

CUT TO:

64   INT. SOUND BOOTH—CONTINUOUS

The AXEMAN sits in a chair looking at the stage.

> DUSTY (V.O.)
> The farmer had a champion bull
> He bred two hundred times a year.
> The farmer's wife said, "Two hundred times!
> Isn't that wonderful, dear?

DUSTY (V.O.) (CONT'D)
Maybe you ought to watch him,
Maybe he'd show you how."
The farmer said, "He's a heck of a bull
But it wasn't all with the same cow."

DUSTY & LEFTY (V.O.)
Bad jokes! Lord, how I love 'em.
Bad jokes! Can't get enough of 'em.
Ooo ooo ooo wee
Bad jokes for me!!

The song ends, to applause. GK comes out onstage.

GK
Dusty and Lefty, the old Trailhands, brought
to you by Jack's Auto Repair. Right back after
this message.

He steps away from the microphone and we hear a recorded
commercial in the background.

CUT TO:

65   INT. FITZGERALD WINGS—SAME TIME

STAGE MANAGER stands in the wings, RHONDA is hugging
him. GK is there with YOLANDA, LOLA, and DONNA.

STAGE MANAGER
This is the first time anybody died at the
show. First time.

RHONDA
We're all getting older, Al.

LOLA
The show's not over, is it?

YOLANDA
He's dead?

STAGE MANAGER
We've got a dead man backstage.

RHONDA
Be glad we don't have one onstage.

YOLANDA
When did this happen?

DONNA
I found him about an hour ago. I walked
away, I dunno, I guess I thought that when I
came back maybe he'd be okay again—

GK
Was he dead when you found him?

She nods.

GK
Where's Evelyn?

STAGE MANAGER
One of the stagehands took her home. She
was all broken up over it. We didn't want
Chuck's wife to run into her.

RHONDA
He was down there waiting for Evelyn when
he passed away.

YOLANDA (BRIGHTENING)
So—

RHONDA
He died with a heart full of hope.

YOLANDA
Not the worst way to go. Sitting in the dark
in your underwear, waiting for your lover to
come rap-tap-tapping on the door.

LOLA
He was in his underwear?

STAGE MANAGER
According to Donna—

DONNA
I don't think we have to tell everything we
know—

RHONDA
He was wearing boxer shorts with
raspberries on 'em and he had a bottle of
massage oil and a bayberry candle burning
and he was playing an LP record of the Mills
Brothers' greatest hits.

GK
He was all set. He was loaded for Evelyn.

LOLA
He was fooling around with the lunch lady?
Mrs. Macaroni and Cheese?

STAGE MANAGER (TO GK)
You've got a couple minutes if you want to
say something about Chuck.

GK
Say what?

YOLANDA
Well, he was on the show for all those years—

GK
I don't do eulogies.

RHONDA
Why not?

GK
I don't do them.

RHONDA
Some reason for this or you just don't care for
people?

GK
I'm getting to an age where if I did eulogies,
I'd be doing nothing but—

YOLANDA
How about a moment of silence?

GK
Silence on the radio? How does that work?

RHONDA
We could sing "Nearer My God to Thee."
Though in Chuck's case, I'm not sure that's
the literal truth.

GK
I don't think so.

LOLA
If my mom died, you wouldn't . . . say
anything? You'd just ignore it? Like she never
existed? How can you do that?

GK

We don't look back, kid. That's the beauty of
radio: it vanishes the moment you do it.
There is no past; we never get old, never die.
We just . . . keep on going.

LOLA
What if you died—

GK
I will.

LOLA
You don't want people to remember you?

GK

I don't want somebody telling them to
remember me.

LOLA is in tears.

LOLA

He died down there. We don't even pay
attention—

GK

The way to pay attention, kid, is to do your
job.

Audience applause as music ends and GK goes out.

CUT TO:

66   INT. ONSTAGE—MOMENTS LATER

Musicians changing positions between numbers.
STAGEHAND moves microphones.

GK
I hope you all had a good time here at the
show—I know we did—and I want to thank
Mr. Chuck Akers for being here and Jearlyn
Steele—

STAGE MANAGER (O.C.)
Great God in heaven—holy shit—

CUT TO:

67   INT. BACKSTAGE—SAME TIME

STAGE MANAGER looks up from his desk, toward the stage.

STAGE MANAGER
What's he doing saying good night? We've
got eight minutes left!!! Lola!!!

LOLA, heading toward the stairs to the dressing room, turns.

STAGE MANAGER (O.C.)
You want to sing a song? Get out there.

LOLA is stunned.

LOLA
Now?

STAGE MANAGER (O.C.)
Now or never.

LOLA grins. She turns and takes off running. She gallops
down the stairs.

CUT TO:

68   INT. HALLWAY OUTSIDE DRESSING ROOM

LOLA dashes down the hall, skids past the door to the
dressing room, comes back, opens the door, disappears inside.

                                                    CUT TO:

69   INT. DRESSING ROOM—SAME TIME

LOLA bursts into the room.

                        LOLA
                       I'm on!

YOLANDA at the dressing table with a stack of CDs, counting
one-dollar bills into a stack, as LOLA rushes to the table and
rummages frantically through a mélange of papers, clothing,
effluvia, in search of a paper.

                      YOLANDA
         Forty-two, forty-three, forty-four, forty-five . . .
         Fifty. You're on what?

                        LOLA
           Onstage. Now. Where's my lyrics?

                      YOLANDA
                    What lyrics?

LOLA snatches up a sheet of paper.

                        LOLA
                      Got it.

LOLA whirls away, then comes back. She puts her hand on
YOLANDA's back. YOLANDA turns. LOLA kisses her lightly
on the lips, a delicate mother-daughter kiss.

LOLA
Thank you, Mama.

LOLA dashes for the door. We hear it slam.

CUT TO:

70   INT. BACKSTAGE—MOMENTS LATER

LOLA comes galloping up the stairs, whirls around the corner
of backstage, through a few musicians who are headed
downstairs, and skids to a stop and glances at the sheet of
paper in her hand.

STAGE MANAGER (O.C.)
You're on, kid.

She looks at the paper in disbelief.

LOLA
Addresses!

(TO STAGE MANAGER)
It's a list of addresses.

She throws the paper away, squares her shoulders, and walks
forward.

CUT TO:

71   INT. FITZGERALD STAGE—SAME TIME

GK
And we'll be hoping to see you back here at
the Fitzgerald next week at this same time—

MOLLY sidles up next to him, her back to the audience.

MOLLY

Six minutes. Lola's going to sing a song. Your
barn door is open.

GK

And in the meantime, we'd like to bring on a
young lady to make her debut on the show.

LOLA upstage from the center stage microphone smiles at the
audience and turns to the SHOE BAND.

GK (O.C.)

You know her mother and her aunt, Yolanda
and Rhonda Johnson—the Johnson Girls, so
she comes from good stock, and now won't
you welcome the very lovely and talented
Miss Lola Johnson.

LOLA (TO BANDLEADER, AS GK TALKS)

You know "Frankie and Johnny were
sweethearts, O Lordy how they could love"?

BANDLEADER (RICH DWORSKY)
What key?

LOLA
No idea.

BANDLEADER
D?

LOLA (TURNING BACK TO AUDIENCE)
Whatever.

The BAND strikes up.

LOLA (SINGS)
Frankie and Johnny were sweethearts,
But he was doing her wrong.
He was doing her wrong in a bad way,
But she was good and strong.
He was her man, but he was a jerk.

LOLA keeps a smile for the audience, but she has forgotten the lyrics. She is making it up as she goes.

LOLA (SINGS)
He was in a hotel with Nelly Bly,
and the gun went rooty-toot-toot
Shot the bastard in the heart
And ruined his nice suit.
He was her man but he was no damn good.

CUT TO:

72   INT. BACKSTAGE—SAME TIME

The STAGE MANAGER's desk.

STAGE MANAGER
Is that how this song goes?

GK
Sort of, yeah.

RHONDA
She always was creative, you know.

YOLANDA
Should I run out there with the lyrics?

RHONDA
Are you kidding? I like it better this way.

CUT TO:

73 INT. FITZGERALD THEATER—SAME TIME

> LOLA (SINGS)
> They took him up to the graveyard,
> And stuck him in the dirt
> Which was very sad
> And the waste of a nice clean shirt.
> He was her man but he was doing her wrong.

LOLA turns to the BAND as they play a turnaround.

> LOLA
> What's the next line?

> BANDLEADER
> No idea.

She turns back to the microphone.

> LOLA
> He had no idea what happened,
> He was waving hello to God.
> He died from eating squirrels,
> And they laid him in the sod.
> He was her man, and he was doing her wrong.

LOLA turns as the BAND plays a turnaround, and MOLLY sidles up next to her.

> MOLLY
> Cool song. Wind it up.

GK moseys out to the announcer's podium.

LOLA (SINGS)
That was Frankie and Johnny
And that's the end of my song.
She put a hose in his tailpipe
Cause he had done her wrong
He was her man, and that's all she wrote.

LOLA howls the repeated last line of the song, in the style of
YOLANDA and RHONDA in "Go Tell Aunt Gladys," as the
audience erupts in applause.

GK
There's a young woman who's going
places—Miss Lola Johnson! And we're going
places, too. We're out of here!

The BAND strikes up "Red River Valley" under him.

GK
Remember to keep your feet on the ground,
your hopes up high, pray for rain, keep the
humor dry, and eat those Powdermilk
Biscuits.

LOLA is joined onstage by JEARLYN, DUSTY, LEFTY, and
other performers.

74   INT. LOBBY OF THEATER—SAME TIME

The DANGEROUS WOMAN walks slowly along the inner
lobby toward the door to the sound booth. She opens the door
and steps in. The AXEMAN doesn't turn to look. She stands
behind him and to the side. Through the big glass window we
see GK and LOLA onstage.

DANGEROUS WOMAN
Show's over.

AXEMAN

You're right about that. Nice perfume. Who
you with? The show?

DANGEROUS WOMAN

I used to listen to this show every week.

AXEMAN

Hey, it was great at one time. But—time's up.
Life moves on.

DANGEROUS WOMAN

It does. So be careful driving tonight.

AXEMAN

You need a lift somewhere?

DANGEROUS WOMAN

There's a shortcut to the airport. A steep hill
and a series of sharp curves and a large oak
tree.

AXEMAN

What's your name?

DANGEROUS WOMAN

Asphodel.

AXEMAN

Beautiful name.

DANGEROUS WOMAN

I listened to them on the radio, they were all
like friends of mine.

AXEMAN

How about me? When do I get my chance?

DANGEROUS WOMAN
Soon.

AXEMAN
How do I find you?

DANGEROUS WOMAN
I'll be right there.

CUT TO:

75   INT. BACKSTAGE—MOMENTS LATER

STAGE MANAGER and MOLLY at the backstage desk.

STAGE MANAGER
Two minutes and you and I can go out and
look for new jobs.

MOLLY
Something in the field of adult corrections,
maybe.

CUT TO:

76   INT. STAGE—CONTINUOUS

GK (SINGS)
From this valley they say you are going;
We will miss your bright eyes and sweet smile,
For they say you are taking the sunshine,
Which has brightened our pathway awhile.

ALL (SING)
Come and sit by my side if you love me,
Do not hasten to bid me adieu,
But remember the Red River Valley
And the one who has loved you so true.

LOLA (SINGS)
Won't you think of the valley you're leaving?
Oh how lonely, how sad it will be,
Oh think of the fond heart you're breaking,
And the grief you are causing to me.

CUT TO:

77   EXT. FITZGERALD THEATER—NIGHT

The black car sits at the curb. The AXEMAN stands by the
open rear door, beckoning, smiling.

The DANGEROUS WOMAN, standing in the doorway of the
theater, smiles, and waves to the off-camera AXEMAN,
declining his offer.

ALL (SING O.C.)
Come and sit by my side if you love me,
Do not hasten to bid me adieu,
But remember the Red River Valley
And the one who has loved you so true.

GUY NOIR (V.O.)
And that was the end of it. Everybody took a
big bow and the curtain came down. And the
Johnson Girls came out for a bow. And that
was it. So long and good-bye.

CUT TO:

77A FITZGERALD THEATER—SAME TIME

Curtain descends the last few inches. Band is playing "Red
River Valley." YOLANDA and RHONDA slip out through the
curtain into the spotlight and smile in the applause and bow
and then retreat.

GUY NOIR (V.O.) (CONT'D)
Except that Lola, who had just made her
debut by murdering Frankie and Johnny,
decided to do an encore.

CUT TO:

78   INT. FITZGERALD STAGE—SAME TIME

LOLA and JEARLYN onstage. They dance, lightly, in position,
in tempo, as the gospel piano strikes up "In the Sweet Bye and
Bye," a slow jazz beat.

LOLA & JEARLYN
In the sweet
Bye and bye
We shall meet on that beautiful shore.
In the sweet
Bye and bye
We shall meet on that beautiful shore.

There's a land that is fairer than day
And by faith we can see it afar
For the Father waits over the way
To prepare us a dwelling place there.

CUT TO:

79   EXT. FRONT OF FITZGERALD—SAME TIME

The black car waits at the curb. The AXEMAN looks toward
the off-camera theater, then leans down to talk through the
open rear door to the driver.

AXEMAN
How long is the ride to the airport?

CHAUFFEUR (O.C.)
Twenty minutes.

AXEMAN
She said there's a shortcut.

CHAUFFEUR (O.C.)
Yes, sir—

AXEMAN
I want to get out of here tonight.

The AXEMAN turns back toward the theater and then climbs in. The black car pulls away, the near rear window rolled down, the DANGEROUS WOMAN in the backseat.

CUT TO:

80   EXT. ST. PAUL STREET—NIGHT

Traffic passes. The old white limestone Assumption church on 7th Street. A few pedestrians pass.

LOLA & JEARLYN (SING O.C.)
To our bountiful Father above
We will offer a tribute of praise
For the glorious gift of his love
And the blessings that hallow our days.

The camera swings slowly around to Mickey's Diner.

LOLA & JEARLYN (SING)
In the sweet
Bye and bye
We shall meet on that beautiful shore
In the sweet
Bye and bye
We shall meet on that beautiful shore.

GUY NOIR (V.O.)
That was the last we saw of him. The car hit
the tree and blew up. Good-bye, Axeman.

81   INT. FITZGERALD THEATER STAGE—LATER

GUY NOIR sits at the piano, playing, a cigarette in an ashtray
beside the keyboard, smoke curling up. The piano lid is down
and the head of F. Scott Fitzgerald stands on it, facing GUY
NOIR. Stagehands are moving the Prairie Home set to the side
and taking it apart. Most of the rest of the stage has been
cleared, but stagehands are still clearing away the drum kit
and monitors and other gear.

GUY NOIR
But it didn't change a thing. They sang
"Sweet Bye and Bye" and the audience filed
out and everybody packed up and left and
fifteen minutes later the demolition guys
were drilling holes for the explosives.
It's just like you learned in eighth-grade
English. . . .

(HE SINGS)
So gather rosebuds, while ye may,
For time is still a-flying,
And this same flower that smiles today
Tomorrow will be dying.

A STAGEHAND stands beside him. GUY NOIR looks up. The
STAGEHAND puts his hand on the piano. Two other
STAGEHANDS stand at the other end. GUY NOIR nods,
stands, picks up Fitzgerald, cradles him in his arm . . .

GUY NOIR (TO STATUE)
Come on, pal. Let me buy you a drink.

. . . and walks away, as the STAGEHANDS move the piano in the opposite direction.

CUT TO:

82   INT. MICKEY'S DINER—NIGHT, A FEW YEARS LATER

A young couple sits at the counter, and an old man a few stools away. Behind the counter, the COUNTERMAN, his back to the camera, pours butter on the grill and tosses on a handful of raw hash browns, and cracks four eggs. He turns to face us. It is the STAGE MANAGER. He looks down the counter toward the waitress who is standing at the cash register, writing in her pad of checks. She is DONNA, the makeup lady.

DONNA
Two scrambled with O'Brien and two to the side with a strip. Double down.

STAGE MANAGER
Two scrambled? I thought you said two up.

DONNA
Scrambled. And two to the side with a strip.

He sighs and turns back to the grill and slaps down a couple strips of bacon and cracks two eggs into a mixing bowl to stir it up.

The door opens and GK, YOLANDA, RHONDA, and GUY NOIR enter, folding an umbrella. The women take off their scarves and fluff out their hair, the men hang up their coats.

GUY NOIR (TO DONNA)
Hey, how's it going? You're looking good.

DONNA

How come you never told me that back when
I looked good?

She nods toward a rear booth. They file past her. GUY NOIR
and GK sit side by side on one side, YOLANDA and
RHONDA on the other. DONNA passes out cups and saucers
and pours four cups of coffee.

YOLANDA

So we're talking about doing a Farewell Tour.

GUY NOIR
Who?

RHONDA

The old gang from the radio show.

GK
Why? The show's over. Been over for years.

GUY NOIR
Who cares?

YOLANDA

I always wanted to do a Farewell Tour. I
loved that last show. I want to do one last
show after another until I'm in a wheelchair
and then keep doing them. As long as I can
still remember the words.

RHONDA

All sorts of towns we never played—
Gooseberry Falls, Lake Winnebigoshish.
There are people in Lake Winnebigoshish
waiting to see us.

GUY NOIR

Well, don't count on me. I got a lot of stuff
going on.

RHONDA

What?

GUY NOIR

Things in the works. Different deals I'm
working out. I'm going to be in and out of
town a lot. The big boys got me jumping.

RHONDA

Doing what?

GUY NOIR

I can't go into all the details.

YOLANDA JOHNSON (TO GK)

How about you?

GK

Fine. I'm just working at the parking ramp.
Free anytime you want me.

RHONDA

The parking ramp??

GK

It's not bad. You get to read a lot.

DONNA approaches.

DONNA

What can I get you?

They look up at her and beyond at the menu on the wall.

CUT TO:

83   EXT. OUTSIDE MICKEY'S DINER—SAME NIGHT

DUSTY and LEFTY cross the street and pass the
DANGEROUS WOMAN, who is standing on the corner. She
turns to watch them walking away.

> DUSTY
> Did she say something to me?

> LEFTY
> You??!!! She was looking at me.

> DUSTY
> Why would she look at you and say my
> name?

> LEFTY
> She was saying, Damn but that is one good-
> looking man.

> DUSTY
> Let's get some grub.

DUSTY heads into Mickey's Diner. LEFTY looks over his
shoulder at the DANGEROUS WOMAN and follows him into
the diner.

CUT TO:

84   INT. MICKEY'S DINER—SAME TIME

DUSTY enters, removes his wet coat and hat, then LEFTY does
likewise.

> DUSTY
> Hey. Long time no see.

RHONDA, YOLANDA, GUY NOIR, and GK all turn to look at
DUSTY as he walks up, then LEFTY.

GUY NOIR
Well, look who came in off the lone prairie. I
thought you left town ahead of the sheriff.

DUSTY
The woman decided not to press charges.

RHONDA
What was the crime? Snoring?

DUSTY
Breach of promise.

LEFTY
We just got back to town from playing
casinos in South Dakota.

RHONDA
Playing what? Pinochle?

LEFTY
Playing our music.

DUSTY
We heard you were getting up a tour.

LEFTY
We've added rope tricks to the repertoire.

DUSTY
Flaming lariats.

LEFTY
It's called Rings of Fire.

YOLANDA
We've got a bus with bunk beds and we're
going back to playing schools and churches.

The STAGE MANAGER/COUNTERMAN walks over, towel
in hand.

STAGE MANAGER
Lola's coming.

He turns.

CUT TO:

85   EXT. MICKEY'S DINER

LOLA climbing the steps to the front door. She is dressed in a
corporate-style suit and carries a briefcase. She pauses on the
top step and turns. She is talking on a cell phone.

CUT TO:

86   INT. MICKEY'S DINER—SAME TIME

LOLA enters, still talking on the cell phone.

LOLA
I'll get back to you on it. The question is
distribution. I don't want distribution. Let
them worry about that. I just want to get our
expenses up front. Expenses plus. Right.
Nine o'clock, I know. I'm on my way. Just
stopping for coffee. Great. Fantastic. Ciao.

As she converses on the phone, she walks toward the booth
where the others sit. She picks up an empty coffee cup and
holds it up, gesturing to GUY NOIR to fill it. He picks up the
coffee carafe, stands, pours her a cup.

                    YOLANDA
She just started six months ago and now
she's the manager of something.

                    GUY NOIR
            What does she do?

                    YOLANDA
No idea. Something in religious software.

                    RHONDA
        It's big. It's moving like monkeys.

LOLA clicks off the cell phone. She sets the briefcase down on
the table, opens it, as GUY NOIR surreptitiously peers inside,
and riffles through papers.

                LOLA (TO YOLANDA)
        I looked at your pension stuff. It's a horror
        show. Ever hear of mutual funds? Honestly,
        you would've done better if you'd stuck it in
        a shoebox and put it under your bed.

                    YOLANDA
    Well, that's why I asked for your help—

LOLA pulls out a sheet of paper and hands it to YOLANDA.

                    YOLANDA
                What's this?

She looks at it.

                    YOLANDA
            Power of attorney?

LOLA hands her a pen.

LOLA
I've got to get your assets working for you.

YOLANDA looks around the table for—what? Advice?
Sympathy? She isn't sure.

YOLANDA
Well, I don't know . . .

LOLA
And you just plunked down six thousand
dollars on a used bus. Why didn't you ask
me first?

YOLANDA
Sorry.

She signs the form and hands it back.

YOLANDA
Can I keep the bus?

She smiles a wan smile for the benefit of the folks around the
table, a smile of humorous resignation as DONNA steps in
with four heaping platters of breakfast and sets them in turn in
front of YOLANDA, RHONDA, GUY NOIR, and GK. The
camera pulls back as LOLA leaves. DUSTY and LEFTY are
perched on the booth opposite, drinking coffee.

LOLA (O.C.)
I'll talk to you later.

The four tuck in their napkins and set in to eat. The camera
looks beyond them to the door as the DANGEROUS WOMAN
climbs the steps to Mickey's vestibule and stands for a
moment at the door, looking in.

RHONDA (O.C.)
That was a terrific eulogy you gave at Old
Man Soderberg's memorial service.

GK (O.C.)
Thanks.

GUY NOIR (O.C.)
Too bad the old coot couldn't have been there
to hear it.

YOLANDA (O.C.)
Yes. And to have missed it by just a few
days . . .

They laugh as the DANGEROUS WOMAN opens the door
and steps into the diner. She stands, looking at them, smiling.
One by one, they look up to see her. They look at each other,
wondering which one she has come for. She steps forward.

THE END

Cast and Characters

Dusty	WOODY HARRELSON
Axeman	TOMMY LEE JONES
GK	GARRISON KEILLOR
Guy Noir	KEVIN KLINE
Lola Johnson	LINDSAY LOHAN
Dangerous Woman	VIRGINIA MADSEN
Lefty	JOHN C. REILLY
Molly	MAYA RUDOLPH
Yolanda Johnson	MERYL STREEP
Rhonda Johnson	LILY TOMLIN
Lunch Lady	MARYLOUISE BURKE
Chuck Akers	L.Q. JONES
Donna	SUE SCOTT
Al	TIM RUSSELL

as themselves:
TOM KEITH, Sound-Effects Man
JEARLYN STEELE
ROBIN AND LINDA WILLIAMS
PRUDENCE JOHNSON

THE GUYS' ALL-STAR SHOE BAND:

RICHARD DWORSKY	Piano, Organ, Bandleader
PAT DONOHUE	Guitar
ANDY STEIN	Violin, Saxophone
GARY RAYNOR	Bass
ARNIE KINSELLA	Drums

with featured musicians:

PETER OSTROUSHKO	Mandolin, Fiddle
BUTCH THOMPSON	Clarinet
Axeman's Chauffeur	CHRISTOPHER K. GRAP
Lobby Usher	DEBBIE DeLISI